BOUND AND BRUTALIZED

"You watch yer mouth, Slocum! What d'you know about Annie, by God!"

"I know she's a real hot lay."

For an instant, rage seemed to paralyze Bruin, but that passed and swift as a whisper he had his big sixgun out. Instead of firing, he slammed it against Slocum's bound arm. The pain burned through him, while the second slash with the big gun lay into the side of his neck. As he felt the chair he was strapped to going down, Bruin hit him in the head...

OTHER BOOKS BY JAKE LOGAN

JAKE LOGAN

SLOCUM AND THE LONG WAGON TRAIN

B

BERKLEY BOOKS, NEW YORK

SLOCUM AND THE LONG WAGON TRAIN

A Berkley Book/published by arrangement with
the author

PRINTING HISTORY
Berkley edition / September 1986

ISBN: 0-425-09299-2

A BERKLEY BOOK ® TM 757,375
Berkley Books are published by The Berkley Publishing Group,
200 Madison Avenue, New York, NY 10016.
The name "BERKLEY" and the stylized "B" with design are trademarks
belonging to Berkley Publishing Corporation.

1

It had been a wet spring, and slow, the snow clinging to the land, ice still edging the river banks in reluctant retreat. Then at last, after the hard winter, the new life was there as it always had been. The earth grew softer, the creeks and rivers filled with snow and ice from the spring breakup, and fresh color painted the stretching trees and the grass. There were flowers, and the land began to sing.

This day the chickadees and jays called, and the sky seemed higher than ever. Those buffalo that were left in the country had dropped their coats, and in the tall timber and valleys game moved with a new vigor over the dazzling land.

In the middle forenoon the strange wagon train

struggled across the valley floor. The horses leaned hard in their harness as the big wheels of the canvas-topped wagons cut the soft ground, leaving testimony to yet another westward passage.

High up beneath the great rimrocks that edged the valley, a tall, broad-shouldered man with raven-black hair and wide-set lynx-green eyes sat his spotted pony. He was studying the passage of the wagon train, weighing the caliber of its leader, wondering why he had picked that particular route which was taking them right into the land of the Sioux and Shoshone. He had already marked the fact that there was no point rider, no horsemen on the flanks; clearly no knowledgeable scout was guiding them through that still unsettled territory. Immigrants, likely, he reasoned; fools, for sure. Just asking for trouble.

At the same time, his attention had caught more than the advancing wagons. The fleeting mirror signal across the valley and the sudden flight of two jays from the clump of bullberry bushes lying almost directly in the route the wagons were taking told him the story.

Immobile on the spotted pony, he was more silent than anything near him. It was in this silence that he listened, his attention acute to every nuance of sound, smell, movement, even shadow. He listened with all the experience of his years with both red men and white, with soldier and civilian; the listening that was the whole of himself, not just his ears, and the looking that was more than his eyes.

Like the Indian, John Slocum knew the difference between looking and really seeing. And like the red man he was patient; he did things slowly and well, and he never hurried. Thus, he was totally quick in a body that carried no unnecessary tension. He was a man who was never contrary to himself, a man with an inner balance supporting the force of a single purpose. He knew who he was; and where.

His eyes narrowed now and he looked away from the wagon train, looked at the deep blue sky to let his face clear. Then he returned to the wagons. *They are arrogant*, he was thinking. *They already come as though they own everything. And soon they will. The Sioux can't stop them. Nothing can stop them. Their contempt and certitude are stronger than all the guns and hearts in the whole of the land, red and white.*

Yellow Horse had said it, and it was true. Yellow Horse had dreamed it, seen it in his vision. Slocum pictured the Shoshone chief and, for an instant, Silent Flower. He quickly put them both out of his mind. Yellow Horse's band could even be near; the Shoshone were not far from the Sioux. Was it Shoshone or Sioux up ahead? he wondered as his eyes went again to the bullberry bushes.

He was also thinking of the riders on his back trail, whom he was pretty sure he had finally eluded. Yet it was still necessary to keep strict vigilance. Because a man never knew. In this country, it was the unexpected that had to be expected.

He allowed another moment to pass, then lifted his reins and began picking his way down the thin trail toward the wagon train.

The long, limp line had stopped, and as he reached the floor of the valley two horsemen came out to meet him. Slocum noted they were riding not-very-good horseflesh as they approached at a ragged gallop.

The smaller man wearing the beaver hat drew rein

first on the hollow-backed bay; his companion, who wore a narrow-brimmed black Stetson, followed suit. He was riding a stockinged sorrel that looked ready for crow bait. They had pushed their mounts over the soft ground, unnecessarily, defining once again for Slocum their inexperience. Greed, he reflected; it was what was winning the West for sure. And he remembered the old Indian saying it: "The whites, they love their God, so they tell us. Maybe so. But they destroy His creation."

John Slocum had big hands, and they were nimble, fast. They could sew a button on his shirt, and they could kill a man. He could rely on them. He kept them close to his weapons now—the bowie knife, the Colt .45, holstered for a cross draw, the Winchester .44-.40 in its saddle scabbard—and waited, sizing the two, saying nothing.

"How do you do, sir." The tone was affable, steeped in cold British courtesy. Those quick eyes beneath the beaver hat glanced over Slocum's face, then down to his waiting hands.

Slocum nodded, including the two of them, but still said nothing. The man who had spoken was wearing a not-very-clean white linen shirt and a black broadcloth coat that had seen more than much use. Wide shirt cuffs revealed a pair of sensitive hands which Slocum thought to be curiously soft for someone this far from town. The man was for sure more gambler than wagonmaster. On his lip hung a full Texas longhorn mustache.

His clipped, dry English voice carried authority, though Slocum was not fooled as he looked at him. The man appeared especially small in his loose clothes, bony, with large, somber eyes beneath which hung deep, dark pouches. There was water gathered in one of his eyes. An easy sixty, Slocum figured.

His large companion lacked any grace of movement, being in a harder body than the smaller man, and living high and tight in his chest and shoulders. He too was dressed in black. But there was something indefinite about him. Slocum had the sense of a man wearing somebody else's clothes. For one thing they were obviously too small for him.

"Know if there's water up ahead, mister?" the man under the beaver hat asked.

And now Slocum heard a difference in the voice as it became less clipped, more nasal; western, in fact. He distinctly caught the snake oil in the words. It was clear to him that they were both pretending, as Beaver Hat slipped back and forth between the English accent of an English gentleman and the loose intonation of a patent-medicine peddler. Interesting. Who the hell were they, anyway? he wondered. Actors? Traveling shows were not uncommon in the Territories.

"There is water up ahead," he said, his eyes taking in the gaunted team of the nearest wagon. "Yonder," he added, nodding. "Past the butte, then to the cutbank and creek. Your horses will find it."

He watched their surprise, and then the man who had not yet spoken said, "Too bad the beasts cannot speak to us." A thin, high laugh broke from him.

His companion did not laugh with him. He was watching Slocum who also had not reacted to the tall man's remark. Slocum took note of that. The man's amber eyes were quick as a bird's. He was surely no dumbbell. Yes, Slocum figured, gambler; but actor too.

"And there is a band of Indians up ahead along with the water," he said, his tone flat.

His words brought an exchange of glances between the men.

"Savages, do you mean? Hostiles?" The hard man with the hard black hat had a big bearded jaw, which he now thrust forward. The beard was cut short, like a spiky bush.

"Depends," Slocum said.

"Depends on what?"

"On how you treat them, maybe. Course, you just happen to be on their land."

"Their land!" The words broke simultaneously from both men.

"This territory was given them in treaty with the United States government. You are trespassing."

"But the army is here! We were told that!" the man with the big jaw insisted. His voice was louder now, and he opened his eyes wide, evidently to emphasize the importance of what he was saying. "They are here to protect us!"

"The army's here to keep the peace," Slocum pointed out coldly. "That means that neither the Indians nor the whites break the law. You, mister, are breaking the law just by being on this land. Not that I give a damn. It is your business."

"Why, to hell with it, I say!"

"Easy, Chimes, boy. Easy." The man with the longhorn mustache kept his eyes on Slocum as he spoke, but his companion heard something extra in the words, for he clamped his mouth shut and closed his eyes.

"My name is Phineas P. Wilfong," the longhorned man said, more British again, and still watching Slocum closely for reaction, but getting none. "Known also throughout the West as Spider Wilfong. This gentleman here is Preacher Chimes. Oliver Chimes. A man of God, as you can no doubt tell. How many Injuns would you say are up ahead there, sir?"

"Enough that you can't handle."

Spider Wilfong blinked twice, while his companion's eyelids, which had been covering his big eyeballs, flew open.

"We were told that this area had been cleared for whites to pass through or settle," Spider Wilfong said, wiping the tear from the pouch beneath his left eye.

"They might only want payment from you," Slocum told him.

"Payment?"

"To pass through their land. Beef. You've got cows."

"And if we don't pay?" Preacher Chimes's hard jaws clamped down on the words.

Slocum shrugged. "You wanted to settle here permanent, didn't you?"

A short silence fell while the incongruous pair took this in.

"But how many can they be that we must fear them?" Chimes said. "The Lord, sir, is on our side! He is not with the heathen! You must surely realize that—and the army!"

Slocum nodded at the waiting wagons. "You've got women and children, have you? My advice—not that you want it—is to haul your ass out of here right now. I said they might be wanting only payment. On the other hand, they might just take the whole kit and kaboodle."

"But . . ."

"Silence!" Spider Wilfong suddenly snapped, turning his head to glare at his argumentative companion. "This is no time to play the fool, Chimes. You are not in the pulpit now; you are right up to your ass in something else." He spat furiously, aiming across his horse's withers, but missing and getting it in the animal's mane.

"Don't you have a scout?" Slocum said. "Who is your wagonmaster?"

Phineas P. Wilfong seemed to straighten a good deal in his saddle. His voice was very British now. "Sir, you are addressing the scout *and* the wagonmaster of this expedition." He pointed his long, thin thumb at his own narrow chest.

"Jesus," murmured Slocum, the word coming forth like a prayer. "Where are you heading?"

"West." At Slocum's sour expression, he added, "We're looking for a place to settle."

"Around here?"

"It is God's country," Preacher Chimes said. "He will show the way."

"You are both plumb crazy." Slocum spat, took up his reins again, and turned his horse's head, giving him a boot in the ribs.

"Didn't catch your name, mister," Preacher Chimes called out cheerily.

Slocum didn't turn around; he simply kicked his pony into a small canter, heading back the way he had come.

The sun was about halfway into the afternoon when he got back up to the rimrocks from where he had first seen the wagon train. They had not moved. He could see a small group clustered by the lead wagon. What could they be doing but jawing it over? The fools! After a while he saw two men—not Wilfong or Chimes—mount horses and start toward the draw that would bring them to the trail leading up to where he was.

He had been watching the bullberry bushes from which the two jays had been flushed earlier that day, but there was no sign of anyone there now. His eyes returned to the wagon train and the two men riding toward the draw.

The damn fools, he was thinking. *The goddamn fools!* The Indians could hit them at any moment, and they were dawdling!

Quickly he mounted the spotted horse and started down toward the two men coming from the wagons. They had wasted too much time already. True, it was none of his business; but on the other hand, that posse might be the type of men who didn't give up easily and could still cut his trail. His spirits lifted. Yes, the wagon train might offer a good cover. Anyway, it was an excuse. The goddamned fools!

2

"I am telling you, the best you can do is get this wagon train turned around and head through Stolen Pass. That is if you're heading west." Slocum spoke the words hard, looking down at them from his worn stock saddle, his forearm leaning lightly on his saddlehorn while he chewed slowly on a stem of bunch grass.

The light was still strong in the late afternoon sky, just at the point where it would turn toward evening. The group of some half-dozen men listened somberly to what the man on horseback was telling them.

"I still don't see why we have to change our plan for a bunch of heathen redskins," Preacher Chimes said, after what had become rather a long silence.

His voice, coming from the pit of his hard belly, seemed to echo across the prairie.

Spider Wilfong cut his eyes fast to the Preacher then, like a bird spotting a worm. "On account of the man says so, you fool. Can't you see the man knows what he is saying, knows his onions, which way the breeze is blowing? I for one didn't come all these sixty years through my hard life to end up scalped and mutilated by some bloodthirsty savages out on the lone prairie." Suddenly he whipped around, almost tripping, but catching himself in time. Lifting his voice, he called to the entire train. "Get 'em moving! Turn them back! We're going a different trail!"

"Jesus," said the Preacher.

"Do not use the Lord's name in vain, Chimes!" snapped Wilfong. "How many times do I have to tell you, for Christ's sake!"

"But we are showing our yellow colors," Chimes argued, spraying those nearest him with saliva, including Slocum's horse, who didn't appear to mind. Chimes spoke fast, the words almost stumbling over each other as they came rushing from his eager, wet mouth.

"Sir...!" Spider Wilfong turned suddenly to Slocum, this time tangling his foot in a clump of sage and coming within a whisker of falling. "Damme!" He drew out the old-fashioned word in dramatic anger. "Damn it! Will you guide us, sir? I was sending those two men out to ask you just that when we saw you riding back down." He was so agitated his gray jowls were quivering.

"You say you're heading this outfit?"

"That is correct, sir!"

"So long, then." Slocum lifted his horse's reins.

"Wait! We need you!" cried Wilfong. "I believe what you say about the redskins, even if my colleague does not! Sir, you have got to get us through! We are on a special mission, and that is no exaggeration!"

"Then I am asking you again who is heading this here outfit, Wilfong." Slocum sat his horse as if he were growing right out of the saddle, even though the animal was wagging his head at flies and sashaying sideways a good bit. Slocum kept his eyes right on the man in the beaver hat.

Spider got it fast then. "Just tell us what to do, mister. We are reading it right along with you." He had slipped instantly into Western vernacular.

"Where are you heading?"

"Like I told you, we're looking for a place, a piece of the Great American West."

Then, seeing Slocum's sour expression, he said, "Feller told us we might take a look at a spot called Medicine Fork. You know it?"

"I have heard of it. Not too far from here." Slocum wondered what they could ever want with such a place, where little happened but weather.

"You say it's near."

"Maybe. On the other hand, it might be pretty damn far if those Indians catch you."

Spider Wilfong didn't even wait a beat. "Sir, we are ready to do whatever you say."

Slocum stood up in his stirrups, his voice booming over the wagon train. "Point 'em north and east! Toward the big butte."

He sat down in his saddle, the pony skittering now under the excitement and the shifting of his rider's weight. Turning the horse, he saw a girl standing at the edge of the group. She had had her eyes on him, he could tell; but she looked away quickly now.

Slocum looked down at the group that was speedily dispersing, reaching their horses and wagons. "The name is Slocum," he said in a loud voice.

A hairy, wet-looking man standing at the edge of the group spoke up in a big voice that all could hear, even the women, who were well beyond the group. "John Slocum, is it." It was more statement than question.

Slocum put his eyes on the dark man as if they were hands, weighing him, feeling the animosity in those words. He was very big, with a wide, flat face. Right now his eyes were as thin as his lips.

"You heard me."

Not waiting to catch the fullness of the sneer in the other's eyes and mouth he kneed his horse, next catching a fleeting impression of flashing blue eyes and jet-black hair as the girl took another look. She couldn't have been more than twenty-three, maybe twenty-four, but those full, firm breasts were for any age, he decided, as the wagon train sprang to life.

"Preacher!" he called down to the hard man with the wide black hat. "You working with me?"

"That I am, Mr. Slocum. I am with you!" The words came in a rush as Oliver Chimes stopped in his tracks where Slocum's words had caught him on the way to one of the wagons. "Give us your orders, Mr. Slocum, and they will be followed! But I must remind you that I am primarily with the Lord!" He ran his big, flat hand over his unhappy-looking face.

"For Christ's sake, Chimes, cut the shit and get with your wagon!" shouted Wilfong from the driver's seat of the lead conestoga. He was standing up, half leaning over his horses' rumps, whip in one hand together with the reins, looking dangerously down his long nose at the Preacher. Flushed with irritation, Chimes managed to keep silent as he climbed into the second wagon and took the reins from a dour-looking women in a black dress.

At last they were pointed in the direction Slocum wanted; and he was glad to see that there was still a good bit of light in the sky.

"Sir," Phineas Wilfong called out, crisp as any British lord releasing an observation, "I understand the redskin does not attack after dark."

"That is just exactly what the last dead man said."

There was the briefest pause. Wilfong's long face split almost in half as his bony chin pointed forward, his mouth almost disappearing. With his eyes squeezed shut, he began to shake. Slocum realized he was laughing.

Then, dropping all the way down the scale into a sowbelly drawl, he laid it out with a spade. "By golly, Slocum, you do know how to fun a feller!"

One of his four bays spooked at something or other and almost yanked his inexperienced driver right out of the wagon, due to the fact that Wilfong had his hand caught in the leather lines. Slocum had a hard time not laughing outright.

His own spotted pony caught the excitement of Wilfong's team and the general tremor of the wagon train as it surged ahead now, and began prancing with impatience to be off and running. Slocum had to take a minute to handle him.

Turning again toward Wilfong, who had just managed to stay in his wagon, Slocum called out, "I want to keep the wagons close together. I want a man riding point, and some flank riders. We'll about make it out of the pocket here before dark."

The sun was almost at the horizon by the time they had left the little valley, a terrible place to be trapped. Slocum had ridden out with the point man, instructing him on what was expected, and had then placed the flankers. Riding back to where Wilfong and Chimes were driving their wagons—the Preacher directly behind the gambler, he noted with amusement—he let his eyes run over the long train.

He had seen the girl climbing into the fourth wagon, but there was no sign of her now as he rode back down the line. His quick eyes assessed each team and driver, the condition of each wagon, and the men who had mounted their horses and were riding alongside. By the time he reached the end of the long line he had a good idea of what he was dealing with.

"Well, how's she look, eh?" Wilfong said cheerily as Slocum rode back up to the lead wagon.

"I'd say you handed me a dead horse and a whip, Wilfong."

Seeing the little man's jaw drop, Slocum didn't wait for a reply. Turning his horse, he shouted, "The flat land up ahead, this side of the creek, alongside the cutbank! Make a circle; turn 'em in a circle!"

The call was carried by the drivers right down the line. Spider Wilfong took it up and was echoed by Preacher Chimes. The ball of sun was at the precise separation of land and sky, and now a coolness had come into the air as they formed to make camp.

"We'll be not so bad off if they take a notion to hit us," Slocum told Wilfong. "That's to say, we will have a chance. With the cutbank and the creek they can't catch us in crossfire and they can't get behind."

His eyes swung slowly along the horizon that was darkening. Nothing was visible, nor did he feel anything special. Still, a man never knew; so, if he wanted to go on living, he never let himself get easy. Not on the trail.

"Camp? Overnight?" Wilfong's jaws were working rapidly as though he was chewing on something. He didn't at all resemble an English dude now. Slocum thought he looked like any whiskey peddler in the Territory.

"I want to see all the men this time. We'll need sentries. And I want to see what weapons they've got. How much ammunition."

"Consider your orders executed, sir," said Preacher Chimes, who had just handed the leather lines of his team to the dour-looking woman in black. He began shouting for the men to come together as he marched quickly around the large circle they had made of the wagons.

Slocum found some fifteen men waiting for him when he rode up to where they were still gathering. He was glad to see that there were some young ones among them, though not many.

"Where are they mostly from?" he asked Spider Wilfong as they waited for a couple of stragglers to come up. "They smell pretty green."

"East. Pennsylvania, Connecticut, mostly, I'd say."

Slocum had his eyes on the hairy giant with the long greasy hair and obsidian eyes who had braced him on his name.

"That there is Felix LeFranc." The purring voice

of Phineas Wilfong came in near Slocum's armpit. "He is one . . . but, I am saying, *mean* son of a bitch, no matter where you cut the deck!"

"I would never have guessed it."

"Him and his friend there joined us at St. Joe. Didn't want them, but I did want protection. Guns. Took a chance for the good of the wagon train."

"Could be they're just what we need," Slocum said softly. "Add some pepper."

"How's that? What's that you're saying?" The little man's chin was racing along with his words.

Slocum didn't answer. He was looking over at the dark-haired girl climbing down from the end gate of one of the wagons.

Spider was right with it. "That there is Monsieur LeFranc's lady friend," he said. He seemed really to enjoy saying it, laying on a French accent. Slocum grinned as he turned to look at Wilfong standing there with his tongue bulging his cheek. "It is Miss Loretta Barclay," Spider went on, "a schoolmarm with a poker straight up her ass."

"Interesting bunch of people," Slocum said wryly, his eyes sweeping the group, which had grown to twenty some.

"I can see you don't figure they're worth much Mr. Slocum; I mean, far as handling teams, horses, and wild Indians. Like that."

"There are a few things that could be better, I'd say."

"But they are willing to learn." Spider Wilfong shifted accent and demeanor again, now from wry observation to the leader with his followers. "They can be taught," he said, and nodded his head up and down a bit like a horse shaking off flies. He sniffed then and scratched deeply at his rear end, his face almost disappearing in all its wrinkles from the effort. Gasping, he straightened, and resumed his survey of the group that was standing only a few feet away.

"See, Slocum, we have got all kinds, all kinds for a town. Just take a look: tradesmen, a barber, an undertaker, cooks for a couple of restaurants, bartenders, carpenters, a lawyer—for land grants and other necessaries." He lowered one lid in a solemn wink. "A doc, a dentist, and, by golly, a schoolmarm, that cute thing you was ogling!" A deep chuckle broke from him appreciatively. "We even got a town council all ready and set up and, by jingo, a mayor!" He blinked his innocent amber eyes fast.

"I wouldn't be able to guess who that mayor would be, would I?" Slocum said, looking at the little man in deep solemnity.

Spider ignored the thrust. "We have even got a preacher. You met him!"

"You have got it all, is what you're saying."

Spider coughed out a laugh. "That is so. Shit, Slocum." He leaned closer, lowering his voice, his damp breath heavy on his companion's face. "Shit, man, I even got the girls. Cast your optics down there to the wagon where that lady is standing next."

Slocum's eyes were already taking in the three young women who were passing some bundles of what looked like washing down from the covered wagon.

"Taking their washing to the creek, maybe?" Cocking his head at the man beside him, Spider Wilfong winked, slowly and full of fun.

"I always did like enterprise in a man," Slocum observed.

"That is just exactly and precisely why you and

me hit it off," Wilfong said. He suddenly took a turn around himself, dancing a caper full of glee and robust self-satisfaction. "Want to know how come I'm called Spider? I'll tell you! On account of I have got more lines out than you can shake a stick at." He gave a huge wink. "We'll set up a game tonight, Slocum. You favor the cards, do you? I believe I am reading you correct."

"At the right moment I do."

Wilfong hooked his thumbs into his armpits and stretched his little chest like a feisty bantam. "We are heading West, Slocum—westering!" Now his accent suddenly became British sterling. "Ah, the Great American West! The land rich with opportunity, not to mention gold, beef, and other enterprises for the forward-thinking man! I am planning a town. Probably at the end of the railroad, wherever that might be. We shall find the right place, never fear. In point of fact, I already have a vague sense of the location in mind." His long thumb released itself from his right armpit and he swept his arm up and around in an arc, signifying infinity. "It all lies ahead! We . . . that is to say, I, Phineas P. Wilfong, have all the necessary!"

His eyes glowed like polished china eggs. "I am not looking for a town that is already established, Slocum; I am bringing the town with me. In those wagons! By God, sir, in those carriers there is everything a man needs to withstand both the frightful difficulties as well as the insane pleasures of civilization and progress."

He paused, his mouth working vigorously, trying to keep up with his thoughts, but only briefly. Then he resumed, in a tone wholly reasonable and an accent absolutely British, as if he were commenting on the weather, the price of wool, or the state of the world. "It is a Master Plan. No question! I don't hesitate to take full credit! The sole thing we lack is protection—reliable gunmen. I do not, of course, mean such as those mangy, disease-ridden, buffalo-skinner types over there, Felix and his companion. But that will come. One must also draw on the local populace, such as it might be, and not rely only on what is imported. Such as yourself, if I may be so bold as to say so!"

Slocum was still watching the three women. Then he turned back to the waiting men. A whole town, by God. All it needed was a locale. Well, why not? Most towns grew piece by piece; Finn Wilfong had his on wheels, all ready to set down anywhere on the prairie where the pickings looked likely. When things got stale, he could simply pack it up and move on. Neat.

Spider was scratching himself again. "Like I said, the only thing we'll be looking for will be protection. But it is actually now that we need it. Now we need the guns. I do not trust LeFranc and his friend Lime. No more than yourself does."

"Where are they from?" Slocum asked, his eyes on the slouching Felix and his buddy.

"Like I said, they hooked onto us at St. Joe when some new wagons joined us, people from Minnesota. Couldn't refuse that lot. Out here, as you know, numbers help against the savages. That one that spoke to you, LeFranc, he fancies himself a gun hawk, and his pal the same. You are going to have trouble there, Slocum."

"Not going to, my friend," Slocum said. "It's already here. But, like I told you, it could put some fire in this pot of stew." He took a quirly from the pocket of his hickory shirt and lit it with a wooden match. "It's about time to show on the betting, wouldn't you say, Spider? I don't see any of them fellers exactly breaking his ass. Maybe they need to see things a little more clearly, huh?" With his thumbs hooked into his wide leather gunbelt, he took a couple of long steps forward and stood facing the group.

"We are close to a couple of Indian tribes, Shoshone and Sioux, and some of them have been following this wagon train for a while. They will take their time. Maybe they'll do nothing, and then maybe they'll hit us tonight, tomorrow, maybe not till the day after. But they will pick their time and place. We need to be ready."

He noticed that the three women had put down their washing and were moving in toward the meeting. Others were coming in too, including the girl Loretta with the jet-black hair and flashing blue eyes, and the young woman who had been standing by the three girls when Spider Wilfong had pointed them out. He was surprised to see that she was younger than he had thought, with a supple body under loose calico. How could he have missed that?

"I want to see all the guns, ammunition, knives, whatever weapons any of you have. We'll need everything we can get our hands on. And we're starting right now on full alert. That means you watch everything. Any of you see or hear anything out of the usual, I want to know it right away."

He had turned his attention back to Felix LeFranc and his companion. "They're not buff hunters," he said, half turning to Spider Wilfong. "They're wolfers."

"Wolfers?"

"They're too dirty for anything but chasing buffalo wolves." Seeing the puzzled look on Wilfong's face he said, "They gut the buffs after the hunters have shot 'em and taken the tongue and hide, and they put out poison for the wolves. It's a shitty job, but they make money. Excepting now in this country it's not good. The wolves are getting real scarce on account of the buffalo are about gone."

"You're saying those two are down here on some other business," said Spider, sharp as a needle.

Slocum, his eyes back on the two wolfers, nodded.

"Thought the Injuns was at peace." The wolfer standing next to LeFranc spoke loudly, and he shifted his weight, spitting at nothing in particular. Like Felix, he was dark, filthy, and covered with hair.

"That's Jake Lime," Wilfong said softly.

"That is what the paper says," Slocum said in reply to the wolfer, speaking slowly and clearly to make sure all could hear. "But some Indians can't read English, and some whites are too dumb to understand it."

LeFranc spoke now as Slocum watched the anger hitting Lime's tight face. "The Injuns is whipped; that's what everybody's been told!"

"If that was so I wouldn't be standing here talking to you," Slocum said. He felt the hot wire running through him as he watched the sneers on those two faces.

"You with the army, Slocum?" LeFranc's little eyes were out of sight, his lids slitted, his contempt collected in the corner of his mouth, where his lower lip seemed to thicken. He stood with his shoulders hunched, like a bull. Ready. Now, turning his head slightly, he appeared to acknowledge the approach of the black-haired girl with a special leer. Slocum quickly read her disdain in ignoring him. If she really was LeFranc's girl friend, as Wilfong had said, somebody ought to let her know, Slocum reflected.

Felix LeFranc was speaking again, since Slocum had said nothing. "How do you know so much about the Injun devils anyways, Slocum! By God, we joined this train to get to the Bozeman, and now you are leading us in the opposite direction. Maybe you be setting us up, by damn!" He nodded his big head toward his companion. "What you think, Lime?"

"Listen to me." Spider Wilfong abruptly cut in with glacial British dignity. "You two men signed on with me as wagonmaster. Mr. Slocum is guiding us away from the chance of Indian attack. So either do as you're told or get out!"

His words gave a moment's surprise to Slocum, but he immediately caught the little man's game. "I will handle this," he said sharply. "Unless you want the three of you arguing with me, Wilfong!"

Spider Wilfong had turned extremely pale. "Just talking, Slocum. Trying to back you. That's all. No offense, old boy!"

"Trying to get the big son of a bitch's ass pokered is what you be doing, Pop!" Felix LeFranc threw back his big head and released a roar of laughter, his companion joining him.

Their laughter was still all over their dirty faces as Slocum took three, four steps forward—swift as a goosed hawk, was how Spider Wilfong later told and retold the story—and the next thing anyone knew Felix LeFranc was lying in the dirt, his face a smear of blood; and then, also as the loquacious Wilfong was to describe it, quicker than a cat's paw, the new wagonmaster had the Colt in his big fist covering Jake Lime.

"There will be no more of that loose talk." The words landed in the group like a couple of dead man's cards. Nobody had anything to argue. Felix LeFranc was numbed; his buddy had frozen in his laughter.

Just as swift as the draw, the Colt returned to its holster. A settling ran through the entire group.

"We will make dry camp," Slocum said. "No fires." He was looking straight at Jake Lime. "And no drinking. You and him—" he nodded toward the fallen Felix. "If there should be a next time, I won't be anywhere near so easy."

As he shifted his weight and started to turn away he again caught the girl looking at him. She hadn't made a move toward her fallen boy friend. So Wilfong had tried to set him up there too. Interesting. *By jiminy,* he was thinking, as the old sourdough used to say up on the Musselshell, *by jiminy, between the pretty girls and those feisty boys, not to mention the wholly untrustworthy Spider Wilfong, things are looking up.*

3

Slocum was wide awake. His hand holding the big Navy Colt tightened just slightly as he lay absolutely still, fully clothed on top of his bedroll. The horse had whiffled softly from the nearby stand of cottonwoods where he was picketed. Slocum listened. Only the animals in the earth now, the slight rustle of wind in the trees, the pulsing of his own body. Externally, he was totally still, yet in inner movement, wholly receptive. It could simply have been something as subtle as a current of air, not necessarily a physical movement nearby. Yet the horse had whiffled.

Still nothing. He continued to lie there with his eyes open, lying on top of the bedroll rather than inside. He had situated himself outside the circle of wagons, not wanting to be trapped in the event of an attack, and at the same time wishing mobility so that he could see whatever was necessary without the camp knowing what he was doing.

Before turning in that night he had scouted the periphery, checking the sentries, telling them what he expected, repeating that they were to report to him immediately if anything appeared out of order. Saddle horses were to be hitched to their owner's wagon; no lights were allowed, no unnecessary sound. It wasn't only the Indians he was concerned with; there were the two wolfers. They would be making some play soon enough, he knew.

Now the moon stood in the northern sky, lighting the earth in clear yet undetailed shapes. The air smelled sweet with that breath of spring that opened a man's body. Slocum felt it singing through him as he lay on his bedding listening.

He had agreed with Wilfong that he would lead the train through Stolen Pass and on down to Medicine Fork. The old man had a map too inaccurate to be of any use, but he assured Slocum that the railroad was building a spur to the area, meaning that Medicine Fork would become a cattle shipping point. That was where he was thinking of planting his town, depending on the conditions they would find when they got there.

It made sense, in a sort of way. If you were in it for the fun, then it made sense, was how Slocum looked at such things. The little man sure had spunk and drive, but he wouldn't trust him as far as he could spit into a Texas blizzard. Now, feeling more familiar with his new wagon boss, Spider Wilfong was assuming the British role less, with usage whittling himself closer to something more essentially his

nature. Thus far, Slocum would have put it as a combination of frontier humor, larceny, and delusions of
grandeur, plus an insatiable hunger for excitement.

His thoughts seemed to have stopped for a moment, and his attention came suddenly together, ring-
ing right through his body as he heard the crackle. It
was a light step, not sure of itself, exploratory, and
he was up on his feet crouched by a bullberry bush
when the figure appeared.

"Slocum . . ." The voice was soft, careful in the
vague night, and not too well controlled.

"Here," he said, listening acutely to make sure
she was by herself.

It wasn't the girl with the black hair and blue
eyes, as his leaping reaction had hoped. To his surprise, it was the woman in the calico dress who had
been standing near the three girls carrying their
laundry.

"Where are you? I can't see." She was a little out
of breath.

"I'm right here," Slocum said. "What can I do for
you, lady?" He holstered the Colt, leaving the hammerthong free, as he stepped out so she could see
him.

He thought he detected a sort of smile on her face
just for an instant. Her next words told him it was
probably so as she said, "I hope I haven't disappointed you. It's only me, not Loretta."

"Loretta?"

"The young lady you were so interested in just
before the meeting started. I couldn't help noticing
since I was watching *you*." Now her laughter came,
quietly, "I hope it's all right my coming out here. I
felt I had to talk to you."

He liked her grave dignity. She must hardly be

thirty; and of course because he'd been so taken by the girl Loretta he'd quite missed her. Yet it was her voice that was especially appealing. It had a purring quality to match her smooth movement, and above all it gave him the feeling that it was really hers, a voice just right for the sadness he saw in her that went with her simple dignity. He found his awakening to her totally unexpected.

"Set," he said, offering her a place on his bedroll.

She sat with her legs tucked to one side, her skirt falling loosely over them; and she sat erect, small-boned in her soft body. In the moonlight he could trace the clean outline of her face and shoulders, and when she turned slightly, her beautifully-formed breasts.

"I am Cassie Wilfong," she said.

"Spider didn't tell me he had such a good-looking daughter."

"I'm his wife."

"Well, he didn't tell me he had such a great-looking wife."

She laughed then, throwing back her head.

"Is that what you came to tell me?" Slocum asked.

She had picked up a twig and was scratching it lightly in the ground in front of her. "I'm not sure I should have come, but I'm here."

He had seated himself on the ground in front of her. "Your husband doesn't know you're here, then," Slocum said, in a tone that indicated he was only saying the obvious.

"Phineas doesn't know I'm here." She raised her head to look directly at him, and he didn't miss the distinction.

After a moment she went on. "I've been with him

. . . a while. I—I've been managing the girls. You saw me with them."

"I see."

"I want to be sure you do. I am their . . . manager, but I am not one of them. And I am their manager because . . . well, he told me those were the conditions. Which I don't wish to go into now."

"So what is it you want to tell me?" Slocum started to take out a quirly and have a smoke, but decided to wait.

The girl seemed to be struggling now. "I don't think I'm being disloyal to Finn when I say that he gets carried away with his big ideas."

"I can see that," Slocum said with a grin.

"But it can get people into trouble."

"People are always looking for trouble, and they're only disappointed if they don't find it."

She was looking down and he thought she was frowning. "Well, you see he's got all those people he's collected; and they're all depending on him to get them through and that they'll start a town and get rich and so on."

"They're not fools. They're most of them honky-tonk, on the make. They've got to be. They're not kids or old widows."

"I suppose. But it all seems such a dream. To build up everyone's expectations."

"You mean yours."

"Maybe. Maybe. I don't know." She raised her head to look at him and he saw that there were tears in her eyes, but not falling. "It could all go bust."

"So they'll throw in and break out a new deck."

"I see."

"What else did you want to say?"

"I guess that's all." She dropped the twig she had been scratching with in the earth, and looked down at her thumbnail.

"I don't believe that's all," he said, and he moved over to sit beside her on the bedroll.

"I should be going . . ."

"Look, I know Spider Wilfong. I wouldn't have lived this long if I wasn't able to figure his kind. But you didn't come out here to warn me about all that."

"What, then?"

He caught the tremor in her voice as she looked up at him, her eyes wide, luminous as they fell over his face, holding now on his mouth.

Slocum didn't say anything. He felt his own desire bursting at his trousers as he put his hand behind her head and drew her to him.

Her body flowed against him. Her lips on his were as soft as her breath, but only for a moment. Suddenly a cry broke from her and her mouth seized his and their tongues found each other. Frantically she began pulling off her clothes, while he swiftly slid out of his shirt and trousers. In seconds that were endless they lay entwined, their naked bodies throbbing, pulsing, pushing.

"My God . . . oh, my God!" Her moans beat against his chest as she grabbed at his thrashing buttocks. She pumped with him faster and faster until her breath was soundlessly screaming in utter delight. Together they came in the exquisite moment that was endless as their bodies pumped slower, squeezing out the very last drops of their joy.

He lay on top of her while her legs collapsed on the bedroll, spread wide. His face was buried in her hair, in her neck, as she continued to moan.

Soon her fingers began to run along the crack of his buttocks and he was fingering her hard, red nipples, which were as big around as his little finger, or so it seemed in his rapidly mounting passion.

"Slocum, my God, oh my God, give it to me again. Please, give it to me again."

He drove down right into the saddle of her crotch, riding now in absolute rhythm with her, faster and faster and deeper and deeper, until the final exquisite moment of eternity when they came together, drowning their organs in the passion that knew no master but its own expression.

She lay on her back, murmuring to the sky, while he leaned on his elbow and looked down at her.

"Slocum, my man. My man!" Reaching up, she drew him down to her, and again her lips were as soft as a butterfly on his. In this manner they played for a while until again his passion rose, in beautiful timing with hers. For the third time they embraced and moved, now more knowing to each other, more aware of the need and timing leading to the exquisite endless dying of their bodies together.

Later they lay side by side looking up at the stars.

"I somehow don't feel worried about the Indians being around us," she said. "I mean, being with you."

"They can be just watching, waiting to see what we'll do. But don't let your guard down."

"Do you ever let your guard down?"

"Out here in this country a man'd be a fool—a dead fool—if he ever did."

"But you make love so beautifully."

"You don't do so badly yourself."

Her laughter tinkled in his ear. "Is that sore, that

scar on your chest? And do you mind my asking?"

"I don't mind. Right now, with your fingers on it, it feels good."

"'You've got a good level head and a no-nonsense way that I like, John Slocum."

"You've got a good level bosom."

"Be serious!"

"You've suggested that Spider doesn't have an especially level head. But that's where you're making a mistake. That old boy could ace the devil out of a free drink."

"Oh, I'm sure. But it's just that; what I'm saying is that he's always manipulating people, and things. Always finagling. You saw what he was trying with you and those two men."

"I saw it, and they felt it," Slocum said wryly. "He tried the same with that schoolmarm."

"Loretta?"

"Telling me she was that wolfer's girl friend. Spider follows the old rule of divide and conquer."

She gave a sudden light laugh. "Do you know how he got all those horses and wagons together?"

"I'd say he won them in a game of stud."

"You really do know him."

"It's my business to know people," Slocum told her.

"That's how he got me," she said. "It was jacks or better in Kansas City."

"Know something?"

"What?"

"I've got a jack right here that's ready for playing."

Her breath was suddenly right up against his mouth.

"You know something, Slocum?"

"What?"

"I'm just dying to play with your jack."

He awakened in the pre-dawn and lay still, watching the faint light of the not yet risen sun coming from below the horizon. He knew now that he had gotten into something deeper than he had at first thought. Nothing wrong with that. But for one thing, it was becoming clear that Spider Wilfong actually had a definite place in mind, and wasn't simply looking about for a likely spot to set up his town. The little man had mentioned Medicine Fork two or three times; he even had a map, nearly illegible to be sure, but still an indication of a definite plan.

Why Medicine Fork? As far as Slocum knew there was nothing there but some deserted shacks and a few bodies. He'd heard of the place from time to time as a played-out mining town, and then a former robbers' roost, a hideout for some of the more notorious road agents and gunmen of not so many years back. A ghost town. Yet, Spider Wilfong was saying that the railroad planned a spur "roundabout that part of the country." It was obvious the little gambler wasn't showing all his cards.

A funny man, Spider. No question but that he could deal quicker than a spitting cat, from his sleeves, from his elbows. A funny man, with his bent for mimicry, playing the British lord, the snake-oil peddler, the old-time local with the sowbelly humor. He was all of those things, and likely more. But mostly he was a medicine-show artist who could slicker the devil into buying a brand-new Bible.

And Chimes. Chimes was fairly straight. Dumb,

but willing; loyal to Spider and a good weapon on his behalf. The others in the train appeared to be more or less the usual drifters who would do anything for a dollar and a little excitement.

Then the girls. Slocum hadn't been impressed by the few he'd seen. He didn't care particularly, as long as Cassie Wilfong was about, and Loretta Barclay. From his point of view, Cassie could have worked all the others into the ground with ease. What a windfall! As for Loretta Barclay, she was stiff as a picket fence. She looked pretty much like she'd been educated in some fancy-pants Eastern school for ladies. Well, he would see just how fancy those pants were.

Yes, an interesting bunch, but real stringy when it came to handling a wagon train, an Indian attack, a storm, or any of the other unexpecteds that always happened on the long trail. There wasn't a useful gun in the bunch. Those two wolfers were the only ones who knew weapons, and he wouldn't trust either more than the other.

Why hadn't the Indians attacked? He had surely seen sign of their presence; he was sure now that they were Shoshone. He had seen it just the night before when he'd scouted ahead for the next day's drive. Still, he was hoping they were only interested in getting some kind of payment, "who-how" beef.

The light was stronger at the edges of the sky as he sat up, and the thought began to form in his mind. Yes, Spider Wilfong was clearly in a hurry. As if he had to get where he was going before someone else did. Was that it?

The sun was still not up as Slocum roused Wilfong and told him to get the men ready to break camp. Then he rode out to see if anything had happened during the night.

None of the sentries had anything to report, but he warned them again that Indians were near. None of them had ever seen a Shoshone or a Sioux, let alone fought any, and only some were even passable horsebackers. As for weapons, a few of the men carried derringers, the standard armament for gamblers. While a few of the girls had their standard, the Smith and Wesson "Lady Smith" derringer which they carried in a handbag. Good at close range, but who wanted to get that close to a charging Shoshone? There were a few Colts, notably the wolfer's; a couple of Henry rifles, and one Winchester.

The day had finally broken clear, with the blue sky shot with pale orange. It was going to be a hot one, he could tell. Just after he had parted with the last sentry, who had been posted on the other side of the creek, he found the bent bunch grass, the horse droppings. And he knew the Shoshone weren't going to attack; not right now anyway. That sentry would have been long dead if they'd had any such notion. There were six of them and they had camped close to the creek, not bothering to hide the fact. Indeed, why should they, so long as they weren't on the path? It was their own country, so why hide their presence unless they were bent on trouble? They could be young braves who had sneaked out of camp for a hunt against their chief's orders, or simply a young bunch who wanted the fun of throwing a scare into some rancher and his family. And the wagon train? It was still a possibility; he couldn't rule that out.

Yes, it would have intrigued them, the erratic behavior of the whites. They would perhaps have figured the travelers were all drunk. And the prospect of whiskey could draw them.

From a high cutbank, and protected by a thick stand of alders, he surveyed the trail ahead, which he had planned to follow with the wagons that very day. The sun was clear of the horizon now, and if Wilfong had followed his orders he would have the wagons rolling. It was time to ride back and meet the point rider. He could see nothing ahead that looked at all suspicious.

It was just as he laid his hands along his horse's nose to turn him that he saw the Indian walking into the creek. Almost immediately a second warrior followed, stepping clear of the willows that lined the bank, while the first had begun to wash himself. In another moment the remaining four entered the water. Obviously they were feeling secure that no enemy was nearby.

Slocum felt certain they were the group that had been following the wagon train. Yet they must know the wagons would now be passing this place, and they were showing no signs of hostility. Was it simply curiosity that had kept them watching the wagon train?

He had taken the field glasses out of his possibles bag and now he studied the warriors more closely as they splashed about in the water. They were little more than youths, and he wondered if their chief or the camp police knew they were out. He had just put the glasses back when he heard the crack of a rifle and saw the young Shoshone take a step, sway, and fall. Two of his companions instantly grabbed him and dragged him to the shore, while the others raced out of the water.

Slocum spun to where the shot had come from, but he could see nothing. And in the next moment he heard the horses down behind the box elders to his left pounding away. He was immediately up and onto his spotted pony, racing after those drumming hooves.

He had cut down a long coulee on the far side of the cutbank and now he broke into open ground that spread like a carpet all the way to the horizon. Far off, too far for him to identify them, two riders raced on dark horses. They were white men. For a moment he considered giving chase, but remembered that the wagon train was his first responsibility. It didn't take any effort to figure out who the Indians would blame for the shooting.

Turning his horse abruptly, he kicked into a hard gallop back to Spider Wilfong and his town on wheels.

4

He had pushed the spotted horse hard, the animal's hooves pounding a drumbeat over the tough ground.

"Follow me in!" he shouted, racing past the point rider.

Spider Wilfong was sawing the reins on the lead wagon, with Cassie beside him.

"Keep 'em moving!" Slocum called out. Wilfong stood up and began cutting the ends of his leather lines on the near horses' rumps.

Slocum rode swiftly down the line, past Preacher Chimes, repeating his order, shouting now for someone to call in the flankers.

Back abreast of Wilfong, he pulled his pony down to a fast, trembling walk. The little animal was sweating and snorting with excitement.

"What the hell's going on?" the old man cried out sourly. "You see Injuns or find gold?"

He handed the team's reins to Cassie, who gave Slocum a quick, though neutral look.

"Come on down from there and we'll talk. Where are those two wolfers?"

"LeFranc and Lime?" The little man's beaver hat moved back on his head as his forehead rose in a nest of tight wrinkles. "I'd say somewhere down the line. You want 'em?"

"I don't see them."

"What's wrong?" Spider had climbed down from the wagon and had untied his saddle horse from the wagon's end gate. It was not an easy job with the wagon moving but much to Slocum's surprise, Wilfong managed without disaster.

Dismounting the spotted horse, Slocum said, "I spotted six Shoshone up a ways, taking a wash in a creek. Somebody took a shot at them. Hit one of 'em in the shoulder, I believe."

"You're saying it was them? Felix and Lime?" Spider was squinting at him hard, his eyes hidden beneath his bushy brows.

"I got a notion. Couldn't see them that close. But I didn't follow on account of the Shoshone will more than likely be hitting the path right now. Especially if that was more than a shoulder wound."

"Shit!" Wilfong had signaled one of the flankers who had just ridden in. "Jess, go find LeFranc and Lime. I want them up here right away."

"Mr. Wilfong, I seen them two riding out early this morning. Heading north." Jess jerked his thumb to indicate the direction. He was a young man with a wildly growing beard and excited eyes.

"Shit," repeated Phineas Wilfong calmly. He nodded at the rider, dismissing him. Then he sniffed, scratching indiscriminately at his small chest, and said, "The sons of bitches have took off." The gravity of the moment had filled his mouth with awe as he uttered this unnecessary statement.

"I do believe they were planted in the train for something like this," Slocum said.

"What do you mean?"

"What I just said. To make trouble. It was no accident they met up with you in St. Joe." He turned with a sudden directness fully facing Wilfong. "Now you listen to me! You want me to get you to Medicine Fork, but you had damn well better start telling it straight to me. I mean, I want the whole story!"

Spider Wilfong was so surprised by the sudden attack that he took a step backward. "Why, I have been completely honest with you, Slocum. If I was a religious man . . . and I'm not even suggesting I'm not . . . why, I daresay I'd swear right on the Bible! I want you to know I have been telling you the honest God's truth of things right along!" The words came clipping out of him like a trotting pony.

"Bullshit!"

"Why, I—"

"You never told me you already had it figured for sure where you were going to throw up your town. You let it sound like you were just sashaying around looking for a likely spot, like *maybe* Medicine Fork. But you had a plan all along, you slick little bastard!"

Spider's bony jaws were racing as he tried to form the words that were leaping to his defense. "True.

True. That is the truth, Slocum, that what you are telling me. I didn't." His agitation had driven him totally to a full Western accent, even to gesture and stance. He stood swing-hipped, low in his pelvis, leaving completely the high British shoulder-girdle grip that made him resemble a clothes hanger, there to support importance and medals. His nose was running.

But this candor, which would perhaps have brought solace from a minister, drew only an oath from John Slocum.

"Someone else is also heading for Medicine Fork, right?" His hard green eyes drilled into the little gambler.

Wilfong nodded, his pale fingers touching his chest in a gesture of feebleness, self-pity.

"Who?" The single word came like a bullet.

"Feller I bested in a game of chance." The words from Spider, on the other hand reached softly, on cat's feet.

"You slickered him."

"I won it fair and square, Slocum. Why, I swear..."

"Won what? What exactly did you win?"

The last wagon was abreast of them now as Spider swept his arm indicating the whole of the caravan. "This! All this!"

Slocum felt something pop inside him at that. He took off his hat and settled it more firmly on his head. "Jesus Christ," he said. "You're telling me you took this whole town in a poker game." He remembered his conversation with Cassie. Somehow he had only thought then of Spider winning the wagon train; but here it was clear that he'd won not only the horses and wagons but the people and, in fact, the whole idea, including maybe even the location.

"Well, actually. . ." Wilfong was the Britisher again. "Actually, old boy, it was jacks or better." He was beaming all over himself. He dropped his eyes modestly. "After all, realize it was the only way I could make my life's dream come true." His lips pursed to emit a soft ditty.

"And the feller you slickered?"

"He managed to take it like a sporting gentleman."

"I find that hard to believe, my friend."

"Well, uh . . . I would have to admit he was a trifle put out by the turn events happened to take. I mean to say, he had a good bit of money tied up in this enterprise." His whole face split now into a icon of charm and good will, even including a touch of sanctity.

"You mean he's looking to bust you right now, likely to slice you north and south next chance he gets. Let me tell you something, Wilfong. Those two wolfers—they are no fun. I know the kind. You're lucky they're gone and you've got only the Shoshone to face."

"It's all a terrible mistake."

"You were double-dealing him, you asshole. What do you expect?"

"He did claim that I was . . . irregular. But it was a lie. A damnable lie."

Spider Wilfong slipped his soft little hands inside his wide galluses, sweeping back the wings of his aged broadcloth coat in order to do so. He began to strut back and forth like a pigeon.

Slocum took out a quirly and lighted it, striking

the wooden match on his thumbnail. "I'd say your former poker companion is pretty damn mad at you. Mad enough to destroy your whole wagon train. That means he isn't interested in it for itself, and he doesn't give a damn for the people in it, meaning he probably has some other plan in mind. You follow?"

"I follow you, Slocum. The clear, succinct exposition of your irrefutable logic is admirable!"

"He will be aiming for Medicine Fork."

"I daresay."

"And you stop the British duke shit, *old boy,* and get your ass back up on that wagon. I've got half a mind to ride on out of here and be shut of the whole of this bullshit."

The words transformed Phineas Wilfong almost before Slocum had finished saying them. "My God, no! Slocum, you can't do that!" He took a step forward, his little hands entreating the air in front of him. "We . . . I need you, Slocum. If those Indians come, we'll be wiped out!"

"That's right."

"But what can we do? What can I do? My wife, all these people. You can't leave us, man!"

"It would be the easiest thing in the world," Slocum said, taking a drag on his quirly. He nodded thoughtfully at the end gate of the last wagon, which was now some distance ahead of where they were standing.

"You wouldn't leave women and children," Wilfong protested.

"I might take the women—the good-looking ones."

"Scoundrel! But all right!" He held up his hand swiftly to stay any words from Slocum. "I have learned my lesson! Sir, you have taught me well! I will do anything you say, but for God's sake, man, don't leave us out here with those murdering red devils!"

Slocum took the quirly out of his mouth and spat reflectively into a clump of sage. He squinted at the quivering man before him. "Mount up, then. Get the word to everybody. Tell them not to shoot at anything, I repeat, at *anything* until I give the order. And from now on, mister, you don't even take a leak without my knowing it. Do you understand me?"

"I do, John Slocum. Oh, I do understand you!"

"Get your ass into that saddle, then!"

The little man was still quivering with agitation. His face was damp with perspiration and his eyes were wide. He seemed almost in shock. "Thank you! Thank you, Slocum!"

In his excitement, his foot missed the stirrup, but he managed to recover and finally swung up into the saddle.

Mounted now on the spotted pony, Slocum cocked his eye hard at him. "One thing, Wilfong. If we do make it to Medicine Fork, this man will likely be there already. Right?"

"He could be, he could be, but I have been hoping to beat him to it. He has no right to be there, since that was part of the deal, that I had first rights."

"What's his name?"

"His name?"

"That is what I just asked you."

"Bruin. His name is Harry Bruin."

Slocum didn't say anything. Spider Wilfong was prompted to ask, "You know him? You ever hear of Harry Bruin?"

Slocum didn't answer. His thoughts were for that instant back in the Silver Dollar Saloon in Jones City, on Carl Bruin spilled all over the green baize-top poker table, his blood pumping into the little derringer that had barely cleared its hideout holster before John Slocum had all but cut him in two.

Things were looking to be even more interesting than Slocum had thought. Harry Bruin was going to be plenty surprised to be running so easily into the man who had killed his brother.

The sun was a pale disc in the heated sky as it reached its zenith. Below, the wagon train struggled across the crackling plain toward Stolen Pass.

"Will we be safe when we get through there?" Preacher Chimes asked, his long face eager for an affirmative response.

"Might be." Slocum had pulled his pony alongside the covered wagon. "Wouldn't hurt you to say some prayers, Preacher."

"I have never stopped, Mr. Slocum. A man of God never stops praying, sir!"

"Glad to hear that."

"You might do well to try it, Mr. Slocum. Pray. I can see that you're a good man." Preacher Chimes licked both rows of his teeth with his tongue after he had said this and gazed at Slocum with wet-looking eyes.

"Preacher, I believe there is a number of ways of saying prayers, you know. Not just folding the hands and closing your eyes."

"There is only one prayer and one Lord to pray to," Preacher Chimes intoned.

"You include the Indians in that?"

"The heathen who can be converted is always welcome in the house of God, sir."

"That is real generous." Slocum spat deftly to one side of his horse and then said, "Now let's hope those Indians you're worried about aren't Sioux."

Oliver Chimes's eyebrows rose on his steep forehead. "You mean, there are some Injuns worse than others?"

"That is correct. Thing is, the Shoshone around this country here are generally peaceable."

Preacher was sucking his gums vigorously as he reflected on this. Several of his teeth were missing due to a drunken brawl he had engaged in at an early age, in which a flying chair had knocked him out of the action. The fight actually had been over the glum-looking woman in black who sat beside him on the wagon, his wife. The story went that Preacher— who by trade was actually a wheelwright—had as a result given up brawling, though not drinking.

"Good thing you be with us, Mr. Slocum." Preacher dropped his voice considerably now so the woman, who was only a few feet away inside the wagon, couldn't hear. "Fact is," he went on, "I had the dislikes for you at the start on account of I had a notion you'd took a yen for my Hester there. . . ." He nodded his head to indicate who he meant. "But I see I was wrong. I do apologize for such thoughts."

Slocum had nothing to say to this surprising confession. At the same time, he felt touched by Oliver Chimes.

He had spent the morning riding up and down the long line of wagons talking to the drivers, the women, and the men riding horseback. For the news of the shooting had spread quickly through the party and all were apprehensive, though in general they were taking it well.

There were a number of wives along, as well as a forty-year-old widow, and a spinster of indeterminate age, though surely past forty. Both had joined the wagon train at St. Joseph. And there were the girls under Cassie Wilfong's care. The social distinctions had eased. At one point Slocum even saw Loretta Barclay talking to one of the "soiled doves." Difficulties and danger invariably drew people together. He knew they would separate again once the skies had cleared.

Cassie Wilfong had smiled at him, their eyes meeting like magnets, and he had felt desire burning in him. Strange, he reflected, how the imminence of danger enhanced sexual hunger. It seemed that way with her too. He only wished there was opportunity to exercise it. One more good reason for getting done with the present mess.

There had been still no sign of any Indian approach by the time they stopped at a creek to water the horses and fill their canteens. Yet Slocum knew they were near. His special sense told him that they were being watched. He said nothing to Wilfong or Chimes; they were agitated enough already, without having their fears confirmed.

He had watered his horse and walked him out of the creek when suddenly he was approached by Loretta Barclay. She was on foot, looking not at him but in his general direction as he rode up a small embankment. Dismounting, he nodded to her, waiting.

She had been riding in a wagon driven by a carpenter named Clawhammer Jones who had only one leg, the other being wooden. Clawhammer and his sister Cora were looking forward to starting a new life in the West. Together they had run an eatery in Folsom Springs, but fire had destroyed the town and being religious folk, they had taken this as a sign. It was clearly the moment to begin again. Loretta had been traveling with the odd pair since St. Joe.

Thus far Slocum hadn't said a word to her. He knew she was aware of him, and had again caught her looking his way.

"Hotter than it ought to be, wouldn't you say, miss?" he greeted her.

She suddenly looked directly at him, as though now seeing him more clearly. He remembered that kind of look from his schooldays.

"I'd say it is, Mr. Slocum." Her voice was cool as water, neither friendly nor hostile. Worse—it was neutral.

"You got something against me, miss?"

He looked directly at her as his words hit. There was a slight change of color in her face.

"Why, no. Surely not. I am most grateful for your taking on the task of getting us to our destination. And if I have appeared unfriendly to you, I do apologize."

Suddenly she smiled at him, a cool, prepared smile; she kept her eyes on his, not backing down. He liked that. He liked the way she handled his question.

"I understand you're planning on setting up a school."

"I have hopes of doing that." She turned then as Clawhammer Jones appeared with some filled canteens slung over his shoulder.

"You ready, Loretta? We'll pull across the creek now. I think the animals have had enough."

"I'm ready, yes." Without a further look at Slocum, she followed the limping man toward their wagon.

Slocum couldn't help feeling that he had been put in his place, and the interesting thing was he didn't mind. He liked the way she had done it. She had class. But as he felt the smile stealing through him, he told himself it was getting to be time to put Miss Fancy Pants in her place. At least, that could be the first order of the day after they got out of the jam they were in.

It had been a good while since he had been in that part of the country, yet he remembered that the Shoshone camp was close. And if they were going to make a move it would have to be soon. The question was whether it would come through their chief or through some of the young warriors, such as the ones who were with the man who was shot. They might simply handle it on their own, disobeying what would be their chief's orders in regard to trouble with the whites. He wondered if Yellow Horse was still the chief, and he wondered how badly hurt the warrior was who'd been shot. He had been fairly sure it was only a shoulder wound, but now he was wondering. It could have been lower; it could have hit closer to the heart. If the warrior died, they were really in trouble. If the Shoshone decided to attack, the wagon train didn't stand a chance. There was nothing they could do other than to keep on moving away from Indian land.

"We'll keep going," he said to Wilfong and Chimes when they asked about making camp.

"You mean all night?"

"Until we get where we're aiming to get."

"But what about the animals? Aren't they going to be tired?"

"The lot of us'll get more rest than we'll want once the Shoshone catch us," he said dryly.

They had pulled through a flat area and were approaching a wide stand of cottonwoods and box elders.

Slocum studied the sky for a moment, judging the weather as the light changed the colors of the earth. The sky was muffled and he could feel the electricity in the air.

"It is fixing to storm pretty directly," he said. And he wished again that there were more guns in the party, and more men to shoot them.

They were almost at the edge of the trees when he saw the war lance with the feathers. It was stuck straight in the ground, directly in their path.

"What is that?" the young man named Jess demanded, riding up to join him.

"Looks like a war lance, I'd say," Slocum replied, cool. He drew rein, holding up his right hand for the wagon train to halt.

"Slocum, what you got there?" Spider Wilfong was standing in his wagon box, leaning back on the leather lines as be brought the four-horse team to a halt.

"I'd say it's an invitation," Slocum said, trotting his horse back to the wagon.

"Invitation? Invitation to what?"

"To not go any farther."

The wagons had stopped and now voices could be heard up and down the line.

Spider said, "What you going to do?"

Slocum couldn't restrain the smile that hit him then. "Funny, ain't it, how when things are going good it's 'What are we going to do' and when they're going bad it's 'What are *you* gonna do.'"

Spider turned his head aside and spat over the left front wheel of the wagon. "Give you a A-plus there, Mr. Slocum. That is for certain true. But the question is still hanging." He grinned, nervously, with no humor at all.

"I guess I'll just have to answer that invitation, my friend." Touching the brim of his hat to Spider Wilfong, and to Cassie, who had just come out from beneath the canvas, he booted his horse into a fast trot.

Except for the herd of antelope, the usual jackrabbits, and a prairie-dog town, the plain lay lifeless under the humming heat of midday.

He knew he was being watched; he had known it ever since he'd crossed the creek by the two low buttes, when he had seen the startled quail.

He rode slowly, carefully attentive to every sound, every movement, every smell. The fresh grass whispered against his horse's hooves as he let his vision widen through the whole of the meadow that butted the edge of the long stretch of plain.

It was a rich day, the smells of crabapple and plum, of wild roses and his sweaty horse filling him; and then, as the meadow ended at the next creek and the land changed again, there was alkaline dust. Now again goldenrod appeared as he rounded a cutbank, and there were chattering chickadees telling him that he was almost there. Even though the silent Indian encampment was still not visible, he could feel its nearness. He could smell it.

And there it was on a high rise of ground protected by cottonwood trees, box elder, and willow. Smoke was rising from the lodge smoke holes and he heard the tinkle of grazing bells in the nearby pony herd. He could feel the watching intensify as he rode closer.

He had not wanted to come; certainly not like this. But it was the only thing to do. And if it was the camp of Yellow Horse, the chief could appreciate that. He would see the action for what it was. Something bold. Not the act of the usual whiteskin. And he would know too who it was riding in.

The lodges were set up in the customary horseshoe, open eastward toward the rising sun. The yellow flowers were everywhere, and the darting bluebirds. A dog suddenly began barking but stopped as suddenly. Yes, they were expecting him. There was, first of all, the unusual stillness of the camp. Where customarily there would be much activity, a great deal of movement and laughter—the children playing and fighting with mud balls, the bigger boys wrestling at war games, the women washing clothes and stirring the cook pot—there was now almost no sound or movement. Nor on riding closer did he encounter the inevitable dogs always present in an Indian camp. It had in fact been that solitary barking just a moment before that had emblazoned the silence.

Still closer now, right into the trees, he began to feel the watching figures almost beside him. Now he did actually see a few, the men staring boldly at him, the women and children with eyes averted.

It was a silence cut from stone.

And suddenly it was Stone right there in front of him. Stone flanked by a warrior on each side. Stone, bareback on a brisk little brown and white pinto, wearing only a breechclout and a bright ornament around his left upper arm. He sat his horse quite like he was part of him—one solidity. His deep, dark eyes were unwavering as he looked directly at Slocum.

There was no recognition, no expression. And Slocum was the same. There was no need for speech. It was no more nor less than he would have expected. Although he was strangely surprised that he had actually come upon Yellow Horse's camp. It was only to be expected that he would run into Stone. Stone, who had vowed to kill him.

It was the Indian on Stone's left who signed, telling Slocum that Yellow Horse awaited him in his lodge.

The chief was alone when Slocum entered. He was seated in front of a low fire of buffalo chips. Slocum took the visitor's place indicated by the warrior who had brought him, who then disappeared. It had been a long while since Slocum had sat with the chief; long ago, up on the Sweetwater, on a day in early spring.

Now, again they sat in silence while the Shoshone chief prepared the traditional pipe and lighted it, lifting a small chip from the fire to do so. Then he passed it to his visitor, and the two smoked in silence.

Presently Yellow Horse emptied the ashes and carefully placed the sacred pipe in its rabbit-fur case.

"Now we can speak with straight words," he said.

"For we have smoked, and men cannot lie when they have smoked together."

Slocum said nothing, his silence being his agreement with what the Shoshone had said.

The chief turned again toward him, his eyes regarding his visitor from deep within him, as though he was looking not with his eyes but through them.

"My warriors are angry. And my people. But my young men are more difficult to control with each outrage done by the white man."

"It is why I have come to see you, Yellow Horse. I had planned to come anyway, even before I saw the war lance standing in the trail."

"I know you, Slocum. You are not like the white men. Nevertheless, not all my people understand that."

The chief spoke slowly, feeling each word and listening to it, while signing with his hands to supplement his poor English.

"I will do all I can to keep the peace between the Shoshone and the whites, Yellow Horse."

"That I know. But will it be enough? It is fortunate that Runs Quickly was not killed. Yet he could have been. He could have lost his life. And the man who shot him is from the wagons."

"There were two of them," Slocum said, speaking slowly, and also signing in order to help the chief's understanding. "They have run away from the wagons. But I will find them. I promise that."

"Who are they? You know them? It is you who have been guiding the wagons. How did you let this happen?"

"I have guided the wagons only two days. These two men, they are wolfers, men who joined the wagons before I came. They are bad men."

The chief was regarding him impassively. "I know you talk in the true way, Slocum. But these men must be brought to me. Not for them to pay you or the wagon people. But to pay me, the Shoshone. It is clear?"

"I will bring them."

"You say wuffers. What is wuffers?"

"Wolfers. Wolf. They follow the buffalo wolves and leave poison for them in the dead buffalo. Then they sell the fur."

"Poison?"

"They kill the wolves with the little pills."

"Then they could kill our dogs, the other animals too. It is a bad thing."

"They didn't come to do that now, to poison. They came to the wagon train to make trouble for the wagon people. It is why they shot Runs Quickly."

Yellow Horse was silent. At length, something like a sigh ran through his body. "The whiteskins are strange."

"I too am angry, Yellow Horse, and I will bring you the two men."

A silence fell and they continued to sit there, feeling each other, each coming to know the other in this special way of the Indian.

Then, without apparently moving, the chief was suddenly on his feet. There had been no effort; it was as though he hadn't even disturbed the air around him, but had expanded into the atmosphere in one simple, flowing movement.

Slocum stood with him outside the lodge for another moment.

"Come back soon," Yellow Horse said. "I cannot hold the angry ones for long."

Without a word, Slocum mounted his horse, which was waiting for him outside the lodge. From the saddle he looked at Yellow Horse again. He knew the chief was an old man, in his late sixties, maybe even seventy, yet he moved with the grace of a small child, and his eyes saw what they were looking at. It was that his life was truly inside him.

Neither said a word. Slocum nodded just slightly, then turned his pony and walked him back down the trail on which he had come. He could feel the chief's eyes on him as he rode away.

Now the silence was even more powerful than when he had ridden in. Nothing. Only the lingering smell of the cookfires. Nothing moved, not even shadows. Nor did the wind sound as it stirred lightly through the trees.

He felt it like hands on him: the fear, the anger. It was not him, he knew. He didn't take it personally. For what else could you expect?

At the same time, he was feeling something else. In spite of the absolute need for caution, he yet had room for that something else. And just as he reached the bend that took him completely out of sight of the lodges he saw the figure. She was all but hidden by the leaves and branches. And he marveled that she had the courage for it. Drawing abreast of the willow where she was waiting he turned his head, careful in case there were others watching. He wanted so much to draw rein, to have just a moment.

And then he had passed her, catching in one fleeting instant those dark brown eyes, and once again the sense of what had passed. It was enough. For the moment it was enough.

Then he was breaking out of the willows and cottonwoods and into the meadow. He was not surprised to find Stone there.

The Shoshone was sitting the same little brown and white pony, his legs hanging down the sides, his left hand holding the hackamore rope, his right hanging loose, not far from the buffalo knife at his waist.

Without a word, Slocum brought his horse to a halt and sat facing Stone. Stone was big for an Indian, with a smooth, muscled body. His skin was like amber satin under which his graceful muscles moved like so many little animals all working in unison, all combining into one highly dangerous and alarmingly swift mountain cat.

"Do you remember, Slocum, what I said the last time?"

Slocum didn't answer. He was watching the other's eyes, his hands, watching too his horse. Stone was every inch the trickster. He was smart, trying to draw Slocum into conversation and rouse his anger. He spoke English well.

"I said if you came again to Silent Flower I would kill you."

Slocum shifted his weight just slightly, listening too behind him. Stone was one of the most dangerous men he had ever met. And the last time he, Slocum, had beaten him. Worse, he had humiliated him, for the beating had been seen by some of the tribe.

"And do you remember what I said to you, Stone?" He allowed a beat to pass. "I said nothing. But you will recall what I did to you."

At his words the Shoshone's eyes became pinpoints, and for an instant Slocum thought he might attack. But Stone was not foolish.

"I know you came to see Yellow Horse," Stone said, speaking slowly. "Yet I am warning you, if you come for any other reason I will kill you . . . with these." He held out his big, muscled hands, bent like an eagle's talons.

"You know as well as I do that when I knew Silent Flower she was not your wife."

"She was my betrothed."

"No, she wasn't. She couldn't stand the sight of you."

"She was my betrothed!"

"You lie!"

As those two words fell into the soft little meadow, Slocum was certain the Shoshone would attack him. Yet it had been essential to make the point clear again, and not let the lie build.

He watched it working in Stone's face and in his body. The man clearly reached the last edge of himself. But Slocum was ready. And just at that moment a calling came from the camp behind him. It was the crier calling Stone's name to come to council.

It flashed through Slocum that Stone could ignore the summons and would attack him. But the Shoshone managed to control himself. He would not go against Yellow Horse. Nobody went against a man such as Yellow Horse, Slocum knew.

For a moment the two adversaries stared at each other, immovable. Even the horses had turned to stone.

"I—I see you again." The words came from Stone on hot breath, just reaching him.

Slocum said nothing. He laid the rein alongside his pony's neck to move him down the trail, with an accompanying kick.

He didn't look back. He wondered whether Silent Flower had been watching. It was a distance across the shining meadow; but he didn't look back.

Fast and high the game opened so that in just moments all thought of Indians or indeed anything at all had passed to the back of everyone's mind; at least everyone who was engaged in the action in Hank Wagner's covered wagon. Wagner was a man with loose lips who laughed, joked a lot, and enjoyed himself; he was especially doing so now as he reached for the bottle of whiskey which during Slocum's absence had swiftly appeared.

"Man does need to settle himself," was how Spider Wilfong put it as he amiably downed a dollop of the good liquor and broke out a fresh deck of cards.

He had allowed Wagner and some others to take in a few pots, just to juice along the game, but now with his poker-polished brain clicking nimbly he began raking in a few big ones himself.

As he pulled in his third big haul, Preacher Chimes smiled all over his strange face. "Ah, but we are noble students of the fifty-two-leaf Bible."

"What the hell you talkin' about, Preacher?" a pear-shaped man with an oval head asked. He appeared simply to have too much skin for his body; and he took up a lot of room in the wagon, even though his shoulders were narrow, for he had very wide buttocks. His loose skin gave him the appearance of being even larger. It fell down from his long face, collecting beneath his chin. Even his hands gave the appearance that he was wearing gloves; they were actually tiny within the two great sacks of veiny flesh. Yet he was not ugly. It was said that he had had three wives, and he still wasn't an old man.

"You could look it up, Porter," Chimes said. "It's an old saying. Use it next time you speak over one of your customers after he's been shot playing cards." Preacher Chimes beamed, his mouth working, and then he said, "Another way of putting it, friend: A pack of cards is the devil's prayer book. Eh?" And he chuckled.

This brought a round of laughter from the group, and Porter Hinds, the undertaker, came out from behind all that loose flesh to smile.

It was most pleasant, Spider decided, relaxing with the boys after all they had been through. Much needed. Very much needed. He dealt easily, with just a slight touch of hesitancy to cover up his adroitness with the cards. No point in frightening people. They were playing for little pieces of wood, buttons, pins, whatever objects were at hand, which had been given certain value in dollars.

Porter Hinds squinted at his hand, his right eye almost totally disappearing as he did so. A soft whistle came through his large lips as he opened for a mythical hundred dollars.

"You're bluffing," said a man named Sorghum Gogh. "I know you, I do. Yer bluffin'!" He was jovial; joshing; ponderous. His heavy accent brought with it fields of wheat, sandringham-blue skies, and milkmaids. He was not long off the boat and had come West immediately, looking for the promised land.

Two players dropped out, Keene and Morrissey. Porter drew one card and opened the bidding with another hundred. Instinct warned Spider to go slowly, not show his ability too soon; but he didn't always listen to instinct when the fire of the game breathed through his small, willing body. And now all stops were pulled when he decorated his hand with three deuces. The deuce was holy to Spider. His lucky card. He already held one. And dueces were wild.

"All right," he said. "I'll raise you a hundred."

But Porter—Spider well knew it—was riding a solid hand. "And up it five more—hundred," the undertaker said, his heavy folded cheeks shaking with excitement.

Now the betting shuttled back and forth between Spider, Porter, and Sorghum Gogh, who was sweating profusely through his coarse pores. His hands were thick, calloused; he was holding his cards like they were a plough handle.

Spider was humming to himself. Porter remained mum, cute with superior knowledge; so he thought.

"Well, Porter?" Spider cocked an eye at him, still humming his little ditty.

"I call, gentlemen. What have you got?"

Porter let out a flutey laugh and fanned his three tens dramatically.

"Ah." Preacher Chimes sighed heavily, having dropped out early. "We shall see that he who is a good gamester is lord of another man's purse."

"It don't look like another man's purse this time, by gum," snorted Sorghum, laying his cards down slowly. "Have a look: three fat queens and a pair of fours. Yah!"

Spider quietly put down his four deuces.

"Glory be to God," said Preacher Chimes, his eyes almost falling onto the cards themselves. "He's

spoked you, Sorghum. Well, if the Lord didn't say it
at some time or other, somebody must have. The
Irish are by heaven smarter than the Dutch!"

"Except that I am not Irish!" snapped Spider Wilfong in his phony British accent.

"Tinhorn!" grumbled Sorghum Gogh. "I might of
known!"

"Watch yer language," snarled Spider, raking in
his winnings.

"He doesn't know the words, Spider," said
Preacher hastily.

"I know that. I know that." Spider smiled benevo-
lently on Sorghum Gogh.

"You teach me sometime?" the Dutchman asked.
"I deal like you, I get to be rich man." He smiled. "I
pay. You teach me."

His face was pure innocence. Spider was about to
reply when they all heard it—the crack of thunder
that shook the wagon. A horse whinnied, someone
called out from another wagon, and as the card
players climbed outside they were greeted by black
skies, and a second tremendous crack of thunder with
lightning zigzagging through the heavens. And now a
deluge of water dropped onto them.

In the midst of it they saw the horseman pounding
toward them. It was Slocum, and he was shouting as
the wind and rain tore at him. "Get the wagons moving. We've got to make it to higher ground. It's a
flash flood. Get them wagons out of here!"

There was water everywhere. As men and women
emerged into the sweeping rain, chain lightning
hissed and burst around them. The air itself smelled
of electricity. Now, all at once a stroke of lightning
illuminated the creek, which had already risen sev-

eral feet. Tree branches were bending under the current. All were aghast at what the brilliant light revealed. Between the bluffs that rose gradually from the stream and the place where they were near its banks, a wide, newly made river spread over land that had been perfectly dry.

In the midst of it all Preacher Chimes was thrown from his horse, landing heavily over a barrel that had somehow rolled away from one of the wagons, his breath knocked out. He fell from the barrel, landing flat on his back with the water running over him, grunting as he tried in vain to swear at his predicament. Dogs were barking. One of them nipped at Hester Chimes, the dour wife of Preacher, as she tried to help him to his feet.

"My God, Slocum!" the drenched figure of Spider Wilfong screamed. "We can't move in this tornado!"

"Get moving! Didn't you hear the guns?"

"Guns! Hell, no, I heard thunder!"

"That was guns. Hear it now?"

The crack of rifles came through the sound of the storm.

"Indians, is it?"

"Who else would be out in weather like this?" Slocum was thinking of Stone. It had to be Stone, the son of a bitch. "They won't hang around if we keep moving."

The storm seemed now to redouble its rage, for which Slocum was grateful. It meant the Indians were also having to fight the weather.

By now the wagons were moving, the horses slipping, the men falling as they staggered around beside them, urging them on. Slocum rode along the line, shouting encouragement, his spotted pony dark with mud as it splashed through the unbelievable deluge.

And then, when he had about thought the storm had beaten the Shoshone, they attacked during a lull. Their rifles had to be useless now, yet there they were, charging through the water. Suddenly a tremendous flash of lightning showed them wavering knee-deep in water, with Stone out in front screaming at them to follow him. The fantastic light now illuminated what moments before had been a green meadow as a roiling lake of black water and debris.

The Shoshone had had enough. Even Stone. Slocum watched them turn and struggle away from the water that soon would have engulfed them.

The animals were terrified, but by some miracle the teams held together, and the wagons now pulled onto higher ground. It was all Slocum could do to whip men and horses into further activity when all they wanted was to wait out the storm, having reached a safer place. But he insisted they move farther away to an even higher elevation. It was past midnight when the storm ended and Slocum ordered a halt. A terrible shocked silence had fallen over the land.

"No lights," he ordered. "I want men for sentry duty. The rest of you get some sleep. Spider, break out that whiskey you been drinking and let the rest of us have some."

Slocum made no attempt to sleep that night, and he met the new dawn with a great relief. It broke fresh and minted over the drenched land. Slocum knew that Stone and his band of Shoshone could also be greeting the dawn with relief. There was no sense in waiting around to see whether they would resume their attack. If the attack had been authorized by Yellow Horse, then they might, but it was more than likely Stone's doing. Yellow Horse, after all, had agreed to Slocum's bringing in LeFranc and Lime; he wouldn't have gone back on his word like this. Stone was probably back in camp right now, covering himself.

Slocum gave the spotted pony a brushdown with a bunch of leafless little twigs, then took another horse, a little bay, and rode out of camp early.

He followed the trail the wagons would be taking, his glance scouring the broad, flat plain. Nothing moved in the early light, and he turned his attention to the dark cliffs lying ahead where they would go through Stolen Pass. But first they needed meat if they were going to make it to Medicine Fork.

He felt good with the tough little bay under him. They found a rough soil pathway leading to higher ground and now moved through a cluster of red spruce, discovering a narrow trail leading through rocks. In a short while they broke into a clearing and he drew rein. In the shallow, timber-fringed gulch a small herd of elk were feeding just beyond some mountain scrub brush.

Slocum waited, sitting his pony while he studied the land ahead and around him. Nearby a ground squirrel streaked across the trail, and he spotted a wild turkey farther down, about halfway to the elk.

As he slipped out of his saddle, pulling the rifle from its scabbard, he felt the quickening excitement running through him. He knelt, measuring the distance, taking careful aim, and time. He wanted only one shot, in case Stone or any other hostiles might be around. Carefully he lined up a young buck and squeezed the trigger. The animal half leaped, then staggered and fell.

5

"Well, I'll be goddamn whang-danged!"

Spider Wilfong half fell off his horse in his race to the ground, stumbled, and nearly landed right on his face, then recovered. Whipping off his beaver hat he slammed it furiously against a big rock at the side of the trail. They were at the lip of a long slope leading down into the valley. Again he struck the rock, dust rising in a cloud from his beleaguered headpiece. "God damn it, God damn it, GOD DAMN IT!" he roared.

His coattails flapped and one of his galluses came loose, the button popping out over the edge of the long draw. His face was scarlet and wet while his flaming wattles flew in indignation. He pranced.

Slocum thought he was going to fall into a serious attack.

They were both dismounted now, Slocum standing beside the little man, who was sucking in air at a terrific rate.

"Take it easy," he said, eyes taking in the long view stretching below them, at the center of which was the cluster of tents, aged shacks, and one or two buildings under construction. The echo of hammers reached them in the clear late afternoon air.

"Take it easy, you say!" Spider began to cough, his face turning almost black, but his rage overcame it and he forced out the words. "Take it easy, indeed! That is easy for you to say! But I—me!" He gasped, sucking his words, his fingers touching his little chest, his throat, and suddenly grabbing at his crotch to subdue a lively itch. "Take it easy! Hah! Do you see what I see, Slocum? By God, do you see that?"

"I am not blind."

"That son of a bitch! I never thought . . . never really thought he could make it! But the weasel, the bugger, has! He has got there ahead of us!"

"Ahead of you, not us," Slocum said calmly.

"But the idea was mine—*is* mine! And he stole it!"

"Who stole it? Who stole what?"

"Whoever that is down there."

"Bruin."

"Harry Bruin, the no-good lout!"

"But you had a notion he might get there ahead of you," Slocum pointed out. "Why are you so surprised?"

"I only *thought*, never really figgered it!" He was glaring down at the little community, his eyes pop-

ping out of his head like knobs. "Shit, I feared somebody *might* just by chance, by goddamn luck, might
get here. Someone might of *heard* something, see!
Was covering my luck like by saying it. But that son
of a bitch! Why, I never in a million years would of
figgered . . .!"

"Don't get so excited. There's always room for
one more."

These calm words almost drove the little gambler
into apoplexy. He coughed, spluttered, broke wind,
belched, and clutched his hands, trying to grab air to
support himself.

"How? How, is what I want to know! How did
that no-good son of a bitch happen to pick on Medicine Fork! He knowed somethin' and he never told
me. The doublecrosser!" His voice faded under the
fury of what he was trying to get out. Then he resumed, slightly calmer, though still speaking swiftly,
his words stumbling over themselves. "See! We was
partners. Briefly! Briefly, let me add for the record!
But it was me knew about this special place. See, he
didn't know about this here. Bruin, he had the fi-
nance, and so he hired the people—it being my idea
—and all the stuff we were going to need. But he
didn't know where it would be."

"And you won it from him."

"Kee-rect! He had the money and I had the brains.
But now, he's somehow got hold of some more
money. But how in the goddamn hell did he figger
out the place, is what I want to know; about the . . .
about it," he ended up lamely.

"Find out about what?" Slocum demanded, boring
right in.

Spider saw he was cornered.

"About the railroad," he said, his voice suddenly new. "About there going to be a spur built. Harry didn't know about that."

"But somehow he found out."

"Exactly."

"Remember Felix and Lime?"

"Those two assholes."

"They were planted with you. Bruin planted them to find out. And they did. You must have blabbed some time or other. That's why they shot the Shoshone. To hang you. Shit, Spider, I thought you said you had all the brains." And Slocum turned his slow eyes onto his companion with his tongue stuck deep in his cheek.

To his astonishment, his companion blushed. His eyes dropped. He shoved his hands behind his galluses and sniffed. "Shucks, Slocum, the best of us makes mistakes. Ain't you never made a mistake?"

"Not *that* dumb."

Suddenly Spider returned to his purpose. "But by God, I have got the land grants. I have got papers!"

"Made out by who? That fake lawyer you got?" Slocum snorted. "If Harry Bruin's got those wolfers' guns and maybe some more with him, I guess you know what you can do with those papers, my friend." Slocum's grin was pretty sly. "You really stepped in it. Well . . ." He turned toward his horse, who had been cropping the short buffalo grass nearby, and gathered the reins and saddlehorn in one hand. "I'll leave you here, Spider. This is as far as I'm taking you."

Spider Wilfong's jaw dropped, and his eyes widened. He worked his mouth silently. In a moment words came out. "What do you mean? You can't leave me out here in this wilderness with all those crazy gunmen about! We ain't in Medicine Fork yet. You agreed to take us right in. We ain't there yet!"

"We're close enough." Slocum leaned on his saddlehorn, looking down at Wilfong. "I don't see any hostiles about—I mean, Indian hostiles."

"But wait a minute! Slocum, I got to think a minute! Now, look, I am needing a lawman for this town. And I planned to offer you the marshal's job."

"No, thanks."

Spider had turned now toward his own mount and was trying to get his foot into the stirrup, but the horse had evidently caught his excitement and was sashaying away from him. At last Slocum reached over and gave the horse a crack on the rump with his reins. The animal stood while Spider made it into the saddle.

"Slocum, you got to listen to me. I got to have time to think, to get settled. See, maybe we ain't right down there in the town, but we *are* the town, this bunch here. We are Medicine Fork, and we will move in." He held up his hand quickly as Slocum started to speak. "There won't be no gunplay. Not when I approach Harry Bruin in a certain way. I know a few things about the man that wouldn't bear repeating. And—and . . ." Again his hand flew up as Slocum started to protest. "I can pay you. I can pay you plenty! I got money stashed, for just such a time. I got good money laid by. I need . . . the town needs you, Slocum. Those innocent women need you," he added, and Slocum caught the slyness in those last words.

"You don't have a town for anybody to be marshal of," Slocum pointed out. "What are you handing me?"

"That place down there, where those old ghost

shacks are still there, all that is in my papers. That is mine. And I want you to show them papers to who-ever it is down there. Harry Bruin or Ulysses S. Grant, I don't give a hoot. I got title!"

Slocum sat his horse quietly, studying the agitated Wilfong, wondering if he was perhaps losing his mind.

"How much do you want? I'll pay it!"

"You don't have that kind of money, Wilfong."

"Gimme a figure. I'll by God double it."

Slocum took his hat off and settled it more forward on his head so that he was squinting at Spider Wilfong from right beneath the wide brim. "I want a thousand down, and a thousand a month with a guarantee of six months. And you don't have to double it. I know you can't meet that."

"Done!" Spider Wilfong suddenly screamed at him. "I'll hand over that first thousand right now. I got it right in my wagon. By God, you said you would and you got to do it!"

Abruptly a silence fell between them, and Slocum knew the little gambler wasn't fooling. Maybe he did have that kind of money. He had named the figure only to shut him up, but, after all, gamblers often did carry big sums.

"I am serious, Slocum. You come to my wagon right now and I will pay you one thousand dollars." Suddenly he was sly. His eyes narrowed, his words slipped out like little eels. "And that cute little Loretta. I see you ogling her. She'll be along. Know that if you be a lawman she won't freeze you out so fast the way she's been doing."

"Old man, you're goddamn nosey, I'd say."

"How about it? Eh? Give 'er a jingle!" His eyebrows arched; he blinked rapidly.

One of the horses snorted and shook his head, his mane flying; the other snapped at a deerfly.

"No fair going back on your word now, Slocum."

By God, Slocum was thinking, *by God, the man means it.* And he thought, *Why not? Why the hell not?* He'd have to face Harry Bruin about his brother some time, and it might as well be now.

"I'll turn it over," he said, and he nudged his horse along his ribs so that he fell in beside Spider's bay as they headed back to the wagons.

Seen from the benchland, the strange town looked like a handful of lost buttons on the prairie. Now, while the sun slid behind the rimrocks, the sky stayed light, covering the earth with a glow. The air was sweet, cooler. As Slocum rode the bay horse down toward the scattered tent houses and shacks, some lights came on. Suddenly a flock of birds swung high above him, gold showing in the tips of their wings.

He heard the hoot of a locomotive coming from the north and west, reminding him that end-of-track was not many miles away. It wouldn't be long before the track layers reached Medicine Fork.

Slocum took his time, riding in slowly and with care. He was thinking what a coincidence if Harry Bruin was really there. He'd never seen Harry Bruin, but he had heard of him. A lot of people had heard of Harry Bruin. Slocum had an idea what he could expect. Old outlaws didn't change their spots. Especially not, by God, when you rubbed out a kid brother. Well, he reflected, you take the cards you're dealt and you play them.

There was only the one street, half a dozen tent structures, while three of the former shacks which hadn't totally disintegrated were in the process of being rebuilt. At the beginning of the street he read the sign nailed to a post that must have once been part of a corral: MEDSINE FORK—WELLCOME

There were two horses at the hitching rail outside the big tent that had SALOON painted on it; a steeldust gray and a claybank sorrel with three white stockings. Slocum swung down from his pony and wrapped his reins loosely around the railing. For a moment he considered going in for a drink. A saloon was naturally the best place to get the hang of a town. But he felt like stretching a bit, so he decided to take a turn on the hard, dusty single street that didn't even have boardwalks. A hell of a mess come a rain, he reflected sourly.

It didn't take him long to cover the town. He walked slowly, smoking the Havana cigar Spider Wilfong had given him on the conclusion of their deal. Slocum had made some changes, notably that he would run for the office of sheriff, since there was no way he could be appointed town marshal without benefit of government approval. But it was possible he could win an election. Meanwhile, he'd keep a protective eye out for Spider, who in turn would handle the election. It was all a good bit loose, but the thousand dollars felt good in his money belt, and he was looking forward to the action.

He smiled to himself as he passed a tent restaurant and the delicious odor of buffalo steak greeted him. A few feet farther on he came to a sign announcing the need for carpenters, and another asking for a tailor and a barber. Halfway along, a peddler selling snake-oil liniment offered him the rights to sell the product at the other end of town. He was surprised to see a livery, also under canvas, but there was no blacksmith, no hotel, nor any real gaming establishment, unless the big tent saloon had something going inside.

It was like any growing end-of-track or mining camp. Rough, functional; though not yet overly crowded. There were cowboys, obviously from nearby ranches, some types who looked like buffalo hunters, but couldn't be since the buffalo were scarce these days, and there were some who had to be prospectors, though the mines were played out. He didn't see any women; a good sign for Wilfong, who would furnish a much-needed service.

The only real difference between Medicine Fork and any other shot-together frontier town was its claim to having once been a hangout for some well-known outlaws. It was a mystery to Slocum how it could ever have been any kind of hideout. He reasoned it must have been a kind of a decoy, for it was completely exposed, naked on the bare prairie. He had a notion that was why it hadn't lasted, that the real hideout had been back in the honeycomb of box canyons that ran off toward the north. Maybe the old Medicine Fork had simply supplied fun and games so the boys could ride in and relax from their strenuous efforts at making a decent living. He wondered if there were any of the old gangs still about. Had Harry Bruin been part of the picture here in the old days? Not unlikely, he reasoned. Interesting, his connecting with Spider Wilfong. Harry's reputation had been with the guns. It was Carl who had really favored the cards. Slocum had quickly discovered how slick young Bruin was, though not slick enough to conceal the fact that he was using a sleeve hideout.

By now he was ready for a drink, as well as any conversation that would fill him in on what was going on at Medicine Fork. Obviously the Big Elk Tent Saloon was the place.

The light was almost gone from the sky now, and in a moment it would be dark. But for a minute or two he remained in the street, which was churned to dry powder, all grass having been long ago worn off by the heavy feet of men and horses.

He had just decided to enter the Big Elk when with a sudden ripping sound the whole tent started to fall, and men came pouring into the street. He had to jump out of the way or he would have been flattened. Shots rang out. Men caught inside the massive falling canvas swarmed across the prostrated wall, and by sheer weight of numbers broke through the top. They were like frantic ants racing out of a disturbed nest, and as fast as they reached the open air, they ran. They darted in all directions, between teams of horses, hurling themselves past people in the street and otherwise making every effort simply to escape the tent. Half a dozen more shots, muffled by the canvas, lent haste to their flight.

Slocum watched in astonishment as the blade of a buffalo knife slashed through the collapsed tent wall and a huge, bearded figure rose through the slit.

"By God, I can tree this here town quicker'n a hound dog can lick his own ass!" the giant roared.

From somewhere behind Slocum a shotgun cut loose and the bearded man let out another roar, though apparently he had not been hit. He didn't linger for a second load, but took off in all haste toward the nearest point of the compass.

It wasn't long before the crowd which had scattered started to return, and thirsty throats turned hands to setting up the tent again. It didn't take long. The poles were raised, the planks which were the bar were placed on upended barrels, and crates, boxes, and barrels were distributed about the premises to create tables and chairs. Somebody broke out a deck of cards. While the restoration was going on, Slocum kept looking for any sign of Felix or Lime, or anyone who might have been Harry Bruin.

Not much liquor had been lost in the fracas with the big bearded man. There was a dead man, however, lying face down on the ground. He was obviously in the way and so two men lifted him by the ankles and wrists and carried him outside. They were back shortly, out of breath and ready for liquid support. No one asked what they had done with the corpse. In only a little while it was as though nothing had happened.

Slocum had seen no evidence of any lawman, nor had any voices been raised in protest over the killing. Maybe nobody even knew the dead man. He stood there sipping his whiskey, idly watching the crowd, which had grown somewhat bigger since the shooting.

Maybe half an hour had passed when the tall man walked in. He was very tall, broad but not heavy, lean and all together like a new whip. He was dressed in riding breeches and wore highly polished Wellington boots. A heavy gold watch chain was slung across his white shirtfront.

Judging from the way he was received, some people nodding and others calling a greeting, Slocum

picked him for the owner of the saloon, or at any rate
somebody important. He wasn't armed. The tall man
nodded here and there, a fixed smile on his face, and
Slocum realized he was aiming toward the spot right
beside him at the bar.

"Pretty dull place without women, wouldn't you
say so?" He had walked right up to Slocum, who was
leaning on one of the planks with his glass in his
hand.

"I'm Clay Chiverton." He held out his hand.
"And I know you're John Slocum."

Slocum ignored the man's hand. He raised his
glass in his left hand, bringing it slowly to his lips.
Out of the side of his eyes he had seen the two men
moving in slowly. They were together for a moment
at the entrance to the tent, then fanned out, LeFranc
going to his left, Lime to his right. And he had the
tall man who was—at least apparently—unarmed,
right next to him. Neat.

Clay Chiverton was clean-shaven and his hair lay
slick on his rather large head, like it had been
painted. He had taken out a small jackknife and was
preparing to clean his fingernails.

Slocum still kept his glass in his hand, but
straightened just enough so that he had a better view
of the three while at the same time he remained fully
aware of the rest of the tent. Easiest thing in the
world to catch his attention on the three while a
fourth backshot him. He was standing now with his
back to the bar, the double planking right against
him, and farther back stacks of bottles and crates and
the wall of the tent. There was just room for the
bartender to move about between the planks and
the canvas tent wall, so he was fairly secure there if

the barkeep stayed out of it. Still, it was possible for somebody to work around behind him if he wasn't alert.

LeFranc and Lime had stopped a few feet away from him, standing well apart, the idea being to split his attention. To his right, Clay Chiverton was standing easy, cleaning his nails. When the two wolfers stopped moving in, he closed the jackknife and slipped it into his trouser pocket.

"I believe you gentlemen have already met," he said in his amiable voice, a voice clear, resonant, and ironic. The crowd opened to allow room for the rapidly unfolding play.

"That is right," Slocum said, equally cool and with deadly humor in his words. "I do believe I wiped the boys off my trail boots somewhere along the way."

He watched the words whip across their faces, LeFranc flushing, while Lime turned a brassy red.

Chiverton didn't let it settle. "Slocum, I wanted to ask you, are you still working for Wilfong?"

"Not that it's any of your business, mister, but I work for myself."

Chiverton lifted his long hand apologetically, a small smile at his lips. "But of course. What I am getting at is how would you feel about taking a job with . . . uh . . . Mr. Bruin? I believe you know the name. Harry Bruin."

The two wolfers had moved in closer, and Slocum watched Chiverton's nose twitch. And now that sense of his whole self had taken over. It was as though he was filled with a cool liquid, and when he moved it was the liquid moving, effortlessly and right on time.

"You did say Harry Bruin."

"The brother of the young man you had an altercation with in Jones City. I believe young Carl failed to recover from the encounter." Chiverton's smile was all over his face. "You're very good at not being taken by your own surprise, Slocum. But I'll tell you, Harry was only too pleased. Carl, his halfbrother, had long been a nuisance to him. And so . . . well, the offer is open. What do you say?"

He saw Chiverton's nose twitch again. "I'll tell you when those two pigs move back a few feet. They're stinking up the place."

This time Chiverton's smile was sour, yet he motioned the wolfers to move back. LeFranc and Lime edged backward, but not very far. They were still threatening.

Chiverton half turned toward the bar. "Another round, Cyrus. For all of us." Then to Slocum, "Maybe you need a little more time to think it over."

"I've thought it over."

"The town needs an honest, upstanding, hardhitting, straight-shooting marshal. A man to keep law and order. We—Harry Bruin and myself too—we are building fast. We need the law."

"I said no, Chiverton. And you know better than that. You know marshals are appointed by government."

"Sheriff, then."

"He has to be elected."

"That is easily arranged."

"I'll tell you, mister. I'm already running for sheriff of Medicine Fork. You got somebody to run against me?"

As the surprise hit Chiverton, Slocum had moved

slightly away from the bar, straightening a little more. He had already slipped the hammerthong on the Colt.

Chiverton, smooth as silk, had turned his surprise into a smile. "You mean you're still getting paid by Wilfong?"

"I mean, mister that it's time you buttoned yourself. And you two . . ." Reaching into his pocket, he drew out a silver dollar and tossed it to Felix Le-Franc. "Go get yourselves a bath, for Christ's sake. You stink worse than a dozen outhouses!"

His suddenly taking the offensive threw the three of them, as he had intended.

"Go fuck yerself, Slocum," Felix LeFranc said, and his hand dove for his pistol.

His fingers froze on the butt of his .44. His face was dead white under dirt as he stared into the muzzle of Slocum's Colt.

"That's not a good suggestion, Felix. The reason I don't kill you right now is I'm saving that for Yellow Horse. Now drop your guns, both of you. Right now!"

Suddenly he felt the familiar tightening inside himself, like something coming together; it was almost a sweet feeling. But he knew it; he trusted it.

And he read it then in Lime's face, the sudden narrowing around the wolfer's eyes, the change in his breathing.

"You tell that son of a bitch behind me to hold it, or the three of you are dead." He drew back the hammer of his sixgun.

Both Lime and LeFranc stood absolutely still. He could feel Clay Chiverton breathing beside him.

"Mister, behind me, you come 'round real slow,

and hold your gun down to the floor. I won't count more than one!"

"Do as he says, Cyrus." Chiverton's voice was smooth and as neatly in place as his slick head of hair.

The bartender who stepped in front of Slocum was totally bald, thin as a stake, with very red hands. In one of his hands he held a bungstarter.

"Drop it right there," Slocum said.

When the bungstarter, a brutal weapon in a bar fight, fell to the floor, Slocum said, "Chiverton . . ."

The man beside him half turned. "Good theater, Slocum. I have to hand it to you."

"Then you can hand me those guns—the wolfers'. Take 'em up by the barrel and lay 'em down here by my feet."

"Don't you think that's being a bit over-dramatic, my friend?"

The shot cracked out instantly, ploughing a hole in the hard ground right near Chiverton's feet. Slocum said nothing as Clay Chiverton bent down swiftly and lifted the wolfers' guns by their barrels and laid them at his feet.

"While you're down there, empty them."

Without a word, Chiverton did as he was told. When he stood up again, he had controlled his face with a smirk.

"Now hand me yours."

Chiverton's eyebrows swept up in surprise. "Me? You can see I'm not armed." He held out his hands in an offering gesture.

"I want that hideout, mister."

The smirk returned as Chiverton reached gingerly into the shoulder holster and brought out the tough-looking little derringer. He was about to toss it to the floor, but thought better of it and, bending, placed it carefully next to the two Colts.

"And empty it."

The tall, thin man broke open the gun and emptied it of its cartridges. When he stood up again he said, "Will that be all, Mr. Slocum?" His words fell out of him like chips of ice.

"Come a step closer."

"Don't you think this has gone far enough, man?"

Slocum's grin was cruel as he reached out, unbuttoned Chiverton's coat, and pulled out the second derringer.

"Now it has."

With the barrel of his gun, he motioned the wolfers to stand to one side. Then he half turned to the bar, took out money, and placed it on the planks.

"Drinks for the house. Anyone tries to follow I'll kill him." He nodded to Lime and LeFranc. "You're coming with me."

"What for?" Felix spat hard on the ground, his whole body tight with anger. "What the hell you think you are, by God, Slocum?"

"I'm the man who's taking you in for shooting a Shoshone up on Little Deer Creek."

"I didn't do it!"

"Move!"

He made it to the hitch rail without any trouble. There wasn't a sound coming from the big tent.

"Where are your horses?"

"Yonder." Lime nodded to a hitch rail across the street.

"Get them."

It was while he was swinging up into the saddle

that he heard the click. The crack of the rifle was within the same second. His bay horse nickered weakly, staggered, and then fell to its knees and rolled over dead.

Slocum had already spun, dropping behind one of the other horses at the hitch rail, firing at where he thought the rifle shot had come from. But it was too wild a chance; he had no target. In the next instant he heard LeFranc and Lime galloping away.

No one had come out of the tent saloon. The drygulcher must have been a guard posted outside by Chiverton. Suddenly a shot cracked into the night and he fired in return. He heard a yelp, then footsteps running. When he reached the corner of the house where the rifleman had been, he found nothing there but a Winchester. It had been close, awfully close. And his two prisoners had gotten away.

In minutes he was down at the livery tent. Throwing money at the hostler, he picked a tough little buckskin and rigged him fast. He was soon on his way.

The buckskin was tough and willing; that was what counted. Slocum couldn't ask more. He was sorry to have lost the bay, but glad it hadn't been his spotted pony, an animal he had grown to rely upon.

Luckily, there was no moon, and so he could travel more quickly covered by darkness. He was being extra cautious, stopping every now and again to listen, to get the feel of the terrain. LeFranc and Lime, and even others could be tracking him, or could even have gotten ahead of him to set up an ambush. He wasn't all that familiar with the country, as they might be.

He felt good about the confrontation in the saloon

tent, glad that the crowd had heard him, seen him backwater Chiverton and his two bully boys. He had established himself, and this was going to be very necessary in the coming days, especially if he really did run for sheriff. At the least, his action now made it easier for Wilfong to bring in his traveling town. There was no official law in Medicine Fork to argue it, and for that matter, the law might soon be John Slocum.

Interesting, the turn of events. He'd worn tin once before, but without enthusiasm. And now too, it would be necessity rather than desire. Although there was something in this whole caper of Spider Wilfong's that appealed very much to his sense of fun and humor. The sheer brass of such an event as Wilfong's town and his own running for a tin badge tickled him.

And Bruin. As a result of the action at the Big Elk, Bruin had lost something of his grip on the fledgling town, and so for sure had Clay Chiverton. But the surprise for Slocum had been Chiverton telling him Bruin was just as glad to be rid of his brother. Was Chiverton telling it straight? Maybe. But even if Harry Bruin hadn't liked his kid half-brother, pride ran thicker than blood. It wasn't so much that Carl Bruin had been killed as it was that Harry Bruin's brother had. That was the point. Revenge so often came from that place. What was clear was that Harry Bruin wouldn't settle for second in the coming battle for Medicine Fork. He was definitely neither the kind who forgave nor forgot.

Nor was John Slocum. There was still the score to settle on Runs Quickly and his promise to Yellow Horse. Moreover, since now LeFranc and Lime would be keeping out of his way, looking for opportunities to drygulch him, he'd have a much better chance at flushing them if he represented the law. By golly, he could even get up a posse. That would be something! John Slocum leading a posse of law-abiding citizens.

And there was the schoolmarm. What was that stiff, poker-backed beauty really doing way out here at end-of-track in a godforsaken place like Medicine Fork? For sure a smart, educated lady like that hadn't come all this way through all this action to teach reading, writing, and 'rithmetic to a bunch of kids.

Finally the third reason why he wanted to hang around. He didn't like that slick, smart son of a bitch with his shiny Wellington boots and his brace of hideouts pushing into just wherever he decided he'd a notion to push. Chiverton. Who was he?

Evidently Bruin needed him. Why? Was Harry Bruin getting to be so old that he had to let someone else run things? Was Chiverton a front for him? People didn't mess with Harry Bruin, Slocum knew. He had a reputation with the sixgun, and it was well earned. The law had never been able to catch up with the old Bruin gang. He had heard tales of Harry Bruin, and he knew it was always good to believe such tales. A man lived longer respecting even the exaggerations. And so why Clay Chiverton?

By the time he had reached the wagon train the sky had been cleared of the few clouds that had come in, and though it was still dark, visibility was better. The wagons lay immobile in the little pocket meadow between the big buttes, as though nobody knew it was there, a place to be found rather than known. It was exactly right for their encampment. There was no sign of movement, though as he approached a horse gave a low nicker and the buckskin replied.

Slocum checked the sentries. Nothing had happened. The men on duty were alert. No sign of Indians, no sign of LeFranc or Lime or anybody. Nothing out of the ordinary had transpired.

He rode softly past Wilfong's wagon, wondering if either of the inhabitants were awake. There was no way of telling—no light, no sound. He continued checking the wagons, the camp, and the area around it. Everything appeared in order, containing the usual disorderly order of a proper encampment.

At length he drew rein at a high place where he had left his bedroll outside the campsite, well beyond the ring of wagons. He dismounted, stripped the buckskin, and hobbled him so he could graze without wandering off. He was unrolling his bedding when something caught him. Slowly he laid the blankets out flat, then raised up and stood stock still, listening.

In the next moment he saw the approaching figure.

"May I come?" She had stopped only a few feet away.

His passion rose instantly. "Welcome," he said. "You've got good ears."

"I heard the horses whinny. I've been waiting."

"And Spider?"

"He's asleep. Well asleep," she added.

He was already helping her undress.

6

The inhabitants of Medicine Fork, Wyoming Territory were surprised in the bright blue afternoon to hear what sounded like the beating of a tom-tom, coming over the sound of saw and hammer from the wooden structures that were going up on Main Street. And when File O'Hooligan, the old saloon swamper and charter member of the town's cadre of heavy drinkers, spurred into town, his lathered horse almost foundering at the hitch rack outside the Big Elk Tent Saloon, his eyes were wilder than they ever had been when boozing and he kept yelling, "Injuns! Injuns, by God, an' headed straight fer town!"

Men had jumped for their horses, had come running with rifles and shotguns and sidearms, stuffing

extra cartridges into their pockets, into saddlebags.
They were all set to light out in the name of Manifest
Destiny and the winning of the West when suddenly
Old Hoss Orwasher had corraled them with the
words, "Shit take it, it hain't the Injuns, it is the
goddamn ignorants! Take a look 'fore you horses'
asses run off making a pack of danged fools of yer-
selfs!"

And sure enough, the beating, trumpeting, and
whistling was indeed coming from what they could
now see was a wagon train approaching from the
southeast; no doubt immigrants, as Old Hoss had
pointed out, but, anyway, nothing to get all feisted
up about. The damn fools were way off course, but
what could you expect from greenhorns?

They were soon to learn that this was no ordinary
wagon train, and that the "immigrants," while certainly green in respect to the trail and the rigor of the
Indian fighting frontier, were to be discovered as
more than seasoned in the arts and crafts of Western
nocturnal pastimes; moreover, not a few saw this
aspect of Western life as fully as important as the
army, the scouts, the hunters and trappers, the cattle
and sheepmen.

Calmer eyes now saw that there were a dozen
wagons moving in good discipline. In place of the
point rider two horsemen rode, one banging on a big
drum, the other cutting some wild notes out of an old
army bugle. The bugler, a one-armed man named
Hampton Deal, knew how to blow his instrument but
not how to play it. Indeed, he looked to be dangerously close to falling off his horse from his exertions.
But he blew loudly enough to raise the eyebrows of
the locals who had stepped out of the dim lighting of

the Big Elk into the bright day of disbelief.

"What the hell is it?"

"It's a circus."

"Thought it was Injuns."

"Injuns don't act that stupid."

"Could be Injuns dressed up, by God, like they do sometimes with the soldier suits."

"It is immigrants. Crazy! And headin' for Oregon, likely."

But then, as the wagons drew closer, someone said, "Hain't that that feller?"

"What feller?"

"That one on the spotted hoss. The big feller what backwatered Clay Chiverton and them two wolfers the other night!"

"By God, if it ain't!"

"By shit, the fur'll by flyin' right directly, once Clay gets to hear of it."

"Reckon."

But the arrival of the wagon train passed smoothly. Neither Clay Chiverton nor any of his gunmen, such as Felix LeFranc and Lime, were in evidence. The general populace was too busy hammering the town together and drinking to do anything but accept the new arrivals. Especially the girls. These were greeted with vast surprise and pleasure. Comments were passed on their appearance and speculations were voiced on the qualifications, but no one was sorry about their arrival. They were a baker's dozen, and someone voiced the view that "By God, they be the best thirteen damsels in the whole of this entire country!"

Spider Wilfong had brought carpenters and these began immediately to erect quarters for the lively business that was expected. Spider meanwhile had his men bring forth canvas and pitch tents with appropriate signs stating the line of business: BARBER AND BATH was one, though the water problem had yet to be worked out; another was LEGAL COUNSEL, JAY PILLTOP; and, of course, Porter Hinds set up as undertaker, Preacher Chimes announced that prayer services would be conducted starting the very next Sunday, and others of varying enterprises followed suit. At the same time, Spider, under advice from Slocum, was careful not to duplicate anything that might already be an established business, unless it was clear that there was plenty of room for an additional service. There was no question about the need for another saloon and gaming establishment. Swiftly a large tent was raised at the other end of Main Street from the Big Elk, with a long bar consisting of the usual planks on upended barrels and crates. The new establishment, which lagged three days behind the Big Elk—indeed, the entire town had only been there about ten days—was appropriately named the Good Time Place Saloon and Gaming Hall.

Close by, cribs were installed for the girls. Cyrus, the bald-headed bartender and manager of the Big Elk, sighed as he watched his competitor taking such a big step ahead in the competition. Yet Cy was a philosophical man. He figured it would all even out in the long run. The Good Time sported a wheel of fortune, a faro dealer, a dice game, and a three-card monte dealer, as well as a number of card "mechanics" as trustworthy house men. Slocum realized how thoroughly Spider Wilfong had thought things through. Cassie, meanwhile, was setting up her girls in appropriate style.

Largely due to the enthusiasm of Spider and his crew, they were accepted right off. After all, the first arrivals had only been there a little more than a week, and Spider's people had brought much that they had by now found lacking.

Clay Chiverton had been all for immediate and rigorous resistance. But Harry Bruin had no intention of opposing the invasion. The intelligent approach, he pointed out, was to absorb and make use of the new arrivals.

"Let 'em get settled, and then we'll see where we're at," the old outlaw was saying as the sunlight came slipping into the cabin window out at the box canyon. It was the morning after the Wilfong caravan had swept into town.

"But they're taking over, and fast," Chiverton protested. "I've been following your orders precisely, but I must say we are losing out on our—or, rather, *your* plan of running the town. We should stop them right now!"

Harry Bruin was shaking his head even before Chiverton was halfway through his words. "Dumb. Plain dumb! Don't you know yet you don't get what you want in this world by going right up against when you can slip around and under? Jesus!"

Clay Chiverton's chiseled nose and mouth looked now as though they had been stretched over his face and glued. Every ounce of him gave off disapproval. But he knew where his bread was buttered and he held his tongue. He had been hired by Bruin as a front man and he was under orders. There was absolutely no question on that score.

The man sitting by the little window of the log

house with the sun washing over his hands and legs,
with his face half in shadow, coughed. He coughed
again, bringing up phlegm. Leaning over a little, he
spat hard at the packed dirt floor. With a sigh he
leaned back in his chair and regarded his "forward
man," as he called him, with amusement.

"You're a bright boy, Chiverton," he said. "In
some ways. But those are the ways we can use, not
the ways where you don't know yer ass from a
pisspot." And he sat there watching the color fill the
younger man's face; his own face was as blank as a
piece of leather.

"You come to me for help, remember? When you
had the trouble with the bank. Wanted to work for
me. Well, I bin teaching you. Do you know that?
This here is your school; a real school that ain't anything like all that book-learnin' shit! Now pay attention. Do you understand that?"

"I appreciate all you've done for me, Mr. Bruin.
I've certainly told you so many times."

"I don't want your appreciation, young feller. I
want you to stop being so goddamn dumb. Shit,
struttin' around like you got a peacock up yer ass and
you don't know shit for Christ's sake!" He spat hard
again onto the dirt floor.

The two now fell silent for some moments, while
these words which had been said so many times during the past year and a half hung in the atmosphere.
Clay Chiverton, former bank clerk, a young man
who had gone to school in the East, a fairly educated
thirty-year-old with a bent for dishonest transactions,
had even so struck Harry Bruin as someone he could
use. He needed a front man. He was too well known
himself for some of his activities, for times had

changed. The old rogue realized it was necessary to keep up with the times. The old days of riding up to a stage with a couple of handguns and demanding they throw down the box were over. Road agenting was almost a thing of the past. And he was getting older. Not as nimble as formerly, when he'd ridden with Harvey Quinn and his brothers, and with the Kid and Sam Topper and such. It was important to change with the times. Use the old noodle, was how he put it in those hideous hours of "training" Chiverton. His apprentice! The word, the thought of it, amused the hell out of him.

Chiverton was improving. He was good with the cards. Carl, the kid brother, had helped there. He, Harry, knew the card mechanic business well enough, but Carl—like that old son of a bitch Wilfong—had something special. Harry's forte was guns, bold thinking, and matchless courage and physical ability. Now, with age, and certain infirmities—old wounds and so on—he was developing his brain. *Never let yerself stop growin'*, was how he'd put it to his pupil.

He relighted his cigar now, blowing a thick cloud of blue smoke toward the low roof of the cabin. Raising his light blue eyes, he regarded the cloud of smoke with pleasure. He was a solidly built man, sixty-some, and only slightly slower than he'd been in the days when he'd run the Bitter Hole gang. Age had hit his legs, and notably his lungs; but it had not at all slowed the gun hand that was swift as quicksilver, nor his brain or ability with the cards. His thoughts turned now to Carl, for Chiverton reminded him of his half-brother. They were close to the same age, or would be if Carl hadn't been so stupid as to

go up against a man like Slocum. Harry Bruin, reflecting on Chiverton and brother Carl, decided that
he admired and liked them about equally. That is to
say, he saw them, as he saw everyone, in terms of
their possible use to himself. Harry Bruin had led a
hard life, and the love that was lost on his family and
acquaintances would have filled a thimble.

"And Slocum," he was saying now, sucking in his
breath to accommodate a sudden clutching in his
chest, a new development which he did not like at
all. But he had no time for a doc now, even if there
had been one about. For there was the Big One at
hand. This was the one that was really going to make
his stake. Something for his good old years to come.
A real stake. Sure, Wilfong slickered him for the
town, but the game was bigger than that. Let that
little Spider son of a bitch crow and cackle; he didn't
have a notion of what he was getting into. And he
was going to let Wilfong and his gang build it, build
the pot, and then he'd just move in with the boys and
take it all. Simple. Thing was—and dumbbells like
Chiverton never seemed to learn it—thing was, not
to allow the indulgence of anger and offended feelings hurt your play.

"And Slocum," he repeated, regaining his breath
as he watched the scowl come into the younger
man's eyes. "He backwatered you, eh?" He began to
shake as the dry chuckle took over and finally turned
into a shout of laughter, but then retreated back into
the chuckle. Eventually the old owlhooter began to
cough.

Clay Chiverton, dismay once again stabbing
through his lean body, stood quite still watching the
old man hack away at his lungs for nearly a minute.
Finally Bruin stopped, his breath hard from his exer-

tion, his eyes filled with water. He leaned back heavily in his chair, his hand reaching down to hold onto the big sixgun at his hip. He felt better then.

"He slickered you and them two assholes."

"The tent was crowded. There wasn't much we could do."

"Bullshit! How many times have I told you, taught you, or tried to, for Christ's sake! You move in close, use yer small gun. A few inches is all you need. Less. Right in the belly. Why the hell didn't you use your sleeve gun!"

"He spotted it."

"He what?" The blue eyes opened wide in astonishment. "I didn't catch . . ." Of course he had, but the pleasure of humiliating his snotty pupil by making him repeat was overpowering. "He . . .?"

"He spotted it. He saw it."

"And he took it off you? Jesus!" He wagged his gray head, which was almost totally covered by the battered gray Stetson hat pulled down tight and almost touching his ears.

Suddenly Harry Bruin stood up. He had moved so quickly that Chiverton had been taken by surprise.

"You're always surprised," the old man said, looking directly at him, and the sneer in his words was like a slap in the face. For a moment the two men stared at each other, and then Chiverton dropped his eyes. He was furious, for he had never been able to hold Bruin's gaze. Now he followed the older man with his eyes as he walked out of the room, leaving the door open behind him. More of his damned arrogance. Clay Chiverton walked over and all but slammed the door shut. He walked to the window and stood staring out.

From the window now he watched Harry Bruin

walk to the round horse corral and untie his dappled gray gelding. He was thinking what an easy target the man made right then. He could easily shoot him, and it could be laid at Slocum's door; or—and it was not a new thought—he could build his reputation as the killer of the great Harry Bruin. But that was dangerous. He would make himself a target then. No, better to use the old man, endure only a little longer his arrogance and contempt, his insults, until he could get his hands on certain papers. And then he, Clay Chiverton, and not Bruin or Wilfong, would call the turn. He would take a leaf from his teacher's book. Let Bruin and Wilfong battle for the town and all the land grants that the arrival of the railroad would make so juicy. He would still do his best job for Harry Bruin, but making sure the matter wasn't settled too soon or too easily. For it was himself who was going to be the winner. Harry was getting to be an old man, while, he, Clay, was still young, in his prime. And Wilfong, though shrewd and even dangerous, was not the power that Harry Bruin still was. He would lose; but Harry Bruin could weaken himself in the process.

Yet there was Slocum. Damn him and what he'd done in the Big Elk. Except that he hadn't really wanted Slocum eliminated so quickly. Slocum, if it was played carefully, could be manipulated into going against Harry, gun for gun. He smiled to himself as he contemplated the successful conclusion of his plan.

He was still at the window, still with his eyes on the fading figure of Harry Bruin as he rode his dappled gray horse down toward the creek and the hidden trail out of the box canyon.

He waited until he was sure Bruin was well on his way, then he too mounted his horse and headed for town.

Not much later he drew rein alongside one of the Wilfong wagons at the edge of town and called out.

"It's Clay Chiverton."

When the girl put her head outside the opening of the canvas, he smiled and lifted his hat.

"I was so surprised to get your message," the girl said. "I had thought you wouldn't get to Medicine Fork until much later than now."

"It is a surprise for myself too," Clay Chiverton said. "Can we talk?" He had dismounted and now held up his hand to help her down from the wagon.

When she was standing beside him she said, "Can you tell me something more about your plans for a school? What you wrote me?"

"We shall have to start it in a tent," Chiverton explained easily. "But we'll get a frame building up right soon. Tell me, did you speak to Wilfong about our arrangement?"

Loretta Barclay looked a little nervous then, but only for a moment, as she thought of Wilfong and John Slocum. Neither of them had any idea that she had been in contact with Chiverton. "No, I followed your instructions. I'm not sure why it was necessary to keep Mr. Wilfong in the dark." She turned her large, luminous eyes expectantly onto the man who had promised her his cooperation in starting a school. The fact that Wilfong had done the same didn't seem at all anomalous to Loretta. She had no idea of the competition that was going on for her services; her whole interest lay in her school.

"I'll explain it to you at the appropriate moment,"

said Chiverton. "Now then, let's get down to business, Miss Barclay."

"I'd certainly appreciate that, Mr. Chiverton."

He smiled slowly, leaning forward just a little, his eyes confiding, his face washed in innocence. "You may call me Clay," he said gently.

Loretta's smile was rather pained as she said, "And you may call me Miss Barclay, sir."

Chiverton had considered trying to stop the parade, but Harry Bruin vetoed him.

"Let 'em go ahead," he snapped. "Let the damn fools hang theirselves."

"But Slocum's going to win. He's going to be sheriff. He'll swamp Golightly."

"What do you expect after what Slocum did to you at the Big Elk, you fool!"

"But we could throw a spoke in their rally," insisted Chiverton, trying to regain something.

Bruin was shaking his head. "You can't change it now. Let them have it, and let 'em wear it out. You can't corral a hurricane, for Christ's sake," Bruin remarked to his companion. They were standing at the window of one of the shacks at the end of Main Street, where Chiverton had set up an office. Harry Bruin was a realist, and he had long since realized that for a determined man such as himself—and damn few others—the only thing that could defeat you was your own old age and infirmities. Rarely did he admit to himself, and never to anyone else, that he was bordering this territory. But the fact that he had lost the game to Finn Wilfong did worry him. It worried him not so much from the point of view of relinquishing property as from his losing his edge, that knife-edge attention and remorseless drive that had carried him—swept him, really—to so many victories. In a word, he was concerned about his aging. And he was even thinking of making this his final caper. After all, seventy—which he would be shortly—was a noble age, and not one to be continuing on the owlhoot trail.

"Who's the schoolmarm you got out here?" he asked suddenly.

"Barclay?" Chiverton was jolted by the sudden question, greatly annoyed that Bruin had been spying on him.

"I dunno her name. I only hear she's good-looking and got a ass like a wedding cake that's got its icing froze solid."

His pupil couldn't stop the laugh that burst from him at this utterance. The old bastard did say some funny things now and again, he had to admit.

"She's come out to teach school."

"Goddamn it, I know that!"

"I spotted her in Denver. Introduced myself. She was on her way to St. Joe to join up with a wagon train going West to settle."

"You mean, my wagons. My settlers."

Chiverton nodded. "And—as we know—she ended up with Wilfong." He felt the flick of pleasure as he dealt the sly stroke. He swept on, before Harry could hit back. "I contacted her again through Felix LeFranc, one of those two wolfers who joined the wagon train so they could spy for me—for us," he amended swiftly. "Wrote her to look me up as soon as she got to Medicine Fork and to keep it all quiet. Not tell anybody."

"And has she? Kept it quiet?"

Chiverton nodded. "I trust her."

"Damn fool. Don't you know by now you should never trust anybody 'ceptin' yerself? And then you'll know who doublecrossed you."

He paused, standing in the middle of the one-room shack. He cocked his eye vigorously now at the younger man. "You had her, have you?"

"Eh?" Chiverton flushed, caught again in surprise.

"I asked you if you'd laid her yet."

"Why, I've only just started to get acquainted with Miss Barclay."

"Bullshit!" Harry Bruin sniffed. "I better look into it myself."

Right then Chiverton would have joyfully killed him. He stared in unfeigned disgust at the broad back, the thick shoulders, and the clomping walk as the old bandit moved to the cabin window.

"We'll see about that," Bruin said, and turned quickly, his hard eyes raking Chiverton's face. "That can wait. We got business to 'tend to." His eyes dug into his pupil. "So stop yer worrying. The old man ain't gonna take her away from you. Leastways, not right now." A cackle like a wild turkey's burst out of his wet lips. This turned into a coughing attack, followed by much spitting and heavy breathing.

"Get that bottle yonder," he managed to say, finally catching his breath. "Soothe the savage. You know about the savage, boy? How many times you been laid? What are you? How old?"

"Thirty."

"Should of dipped yer wick plenty by age thirty."

Chiverton grinned, humoring the old man. "I've done my share."

Both drank to this. The liquor had its effect,

served its purpose; the pair loosened.

Harry Bruin said, as he slipped comfortably into his chair and put his feet up on a wooden chest, "Practice makes perfect. Same with the women." He grinned, his lips wet with pleasure as his eyes danced. "Course, don't never let yerself get to be perfect at it, boy."

"Why not?" Chiverton asked in surprise. "Isn't that the whole idea?"

Harry Bruin, loving the role of teacher and sage, began to shake in silent laughter even before Chiverton finished his sentence. "Perfect, eh? You young jackanapes, none of you got any idea of what the hell goes on in this man's world. Perfect! Hah! Shit, I am telling you, it's only a fool gets hisself perfect with the women. Hell, then you wouldn't need to practice any more, now would you!" And he collapsed in laughter, nearly dropping his drink, roaring with mirth, falling into a wet attack of coughing, until finally, limp and exhausted, his breath wheezing, he leaned back and raised his glass weakly to his trembling lips.

"Here. Drink up. Drink to life. Hell, it's all we got, and by God it's all a man needs!"

Slocum had witnessed a certain number of parades and other political shenanigans in his time, but the show put on by Spider Wilfong and his boys had to be one of the memorable events that he would not soon forget.

It wasn't long past nightfall when Main Street began to fill with people. There were no street lights in the town, but there was a bright moon, and the lights from several tents beamed forth to help illuminate the great moment. Nor was there only the moon above. The entire sky was dotted and dusted with stars. In no time the town seemed to be overflowing.

The crowd was noisy, aided and abetted—under Spider Wilfong's instructions—by the musicians from the Big Elk and the Good Time Place Saloon and Gaming Hall. From these emporiums of pleasure came the fiddled strains of "Chicken in the Breadtray," "Old Dan Tucker," and "The Irish Washerwoman." Accompanied by the clomping of heavy boots, shouts, wolf calls, whistles, and curses, the activity reaching an astounding pitch. Spider's and Cassie's girls had certainly brought life to Medicine Fork, Slocum decided, as he listened to the "do-se-do" of the caller rising above the shindig.

Now both saloons began to empty as a drum was heard coming down the street, accompanied by the uncontrolled bugle of Hampton Deal. Men were in some sort of formation now, many of them carrying torches. The bass drum could be heard, louder now, accompanied by a fife, banjos, and fiddles. Old Terwilliger Fanning, a former wrestler, led the band, sawing elaborately on a fiddle as he danced wildly along the street. Right behind him came Heavy Hank Wagner, his cheeks puffed out like balls as he blew on a cornet. There was a tumbler and a pretty inexperienced juggler, but nobody minded their amateurism. All wondered where in the devil Wilfong, the redoubtable Spider, had dug up all these marvelous incompetents and welded them in an instant into one of the best parades anybody had ever seen.

Right in the very center of it all was Spider Wilfong himself—in person!—wearing a huge Texas hat with a brim as wide as the roof of a house, his great longhorn mustache waxed into infinity at the points, and riding a shining white horse. Every few steps this fabulous apparition whipped off his hat and waved it at the crowd, bellowing at them to vote for John Slocum in the morning. Then, turning to those nearest him in the parade, notably Preacher Chimes and Cassie, he cursed Slocum for refusing to lead the carnival himself. Yet, it would have killed Spider— as indeed anyone would have agreed—if anyone but himself had taken center stage. Slocum had wisely realized this, and Spider raised him another notch in his estimation.

Meanwhile, to Slocum's surprise and delight, he discovered that Spider had placed shills amongst the crowd informing all of the men that a vote for John Slocum would guarantee a free engagement with one of the girls at the Good Time Place Saloon and Gaming Hall. How could he lose? Slocum was thinking. He mentally took off his hat to Phineas P. Wilfong, wondering what the P stood for—piss and vinegar?

"A vote for John Slocum is a vote for law and order!" Spider shouted above the tumult of fire-lighted, sweating faces, the thudding of the big drum, and the neighing of excited horses.

"It is a vote for a man with the God-given right of honesty and conscience," intoned Preacher Chimes. "Vote for this God-fearing man and you will be able to sleep safely in your homes at night!"

At the end of these noble words, he suddenly whipped out an American flag from inside his coat and waved it wildly at the crowd. The sudden action served to spook his horse, a big sorrel gelding, and it began to buck, to the vast delight of the onlookers, who urged the reverend to "ride 'im cowboy!" But the Preacher was grabbing leather and air for all he was worth. Suddenly he went flying, to land spreadeagled in a wagon box which had in it some open sacks of flour. The crowd roared with delight as Chimes rose, fortunately unhurt, covered with flour and looking like an astonished ghost.

Spider had planned a speech, but he found that when the parade came to a halt and he prepared to deliver his words, nobody wanted to listen. Manfully overcoming a struggle with his feelings on the matter, he had sense enough, Slocum was pleased to note, to go with what best suited the moment. "Drinks for everyone at the Good Time!" he suddenly shouted, whipping off his enormous Texas hat. Midway, he suddenly remembered the fate of Preacher Chimes and stopped. Bowing his head, the great hat covering not only his heart but almost the whole of himself, he prayed aloud for victory at the ballot box. Following this devotional exercise, he dismounted sorely and made his way into the Good Time.

"It's costing the little bastard a fortune," Harry Bruin observed to his companion as they watched the parade from the office window in town. "He thinks he's got it all now."

"He hasn't got me," his companion said sweetly.

Harry Bruin turned to the tall blonde and smiled, realizing as he did so that lately he hadn't smiled much at all. "You bet that cute little ass of yours he hasn't," he said, slipping his arm around her waist.

"I'm so glad you brought me to town. I was getting a little crazy out there in that canyon."

"It won't be much longer. Then we'll head for some good times." His hand slipped down to her buttocks.

"If you keep that up, Mr. Bruin, we'll be having our good times right now," she said, her breath catching.

He drew her away from the window now and, placing his hands on her shoulders, pushed her down. She didn't need any encouragement, but dropped instantly to her knees, her fingers working at his fly.

In a moment she had it out and in her fist.

"Kiss it," he whispered throatily.

Her tongue flicked out to lick the end of his rigid member.

"My God," he gasped, feeling his knees starting to buckle.

"Harry . . . Harry . . ."

"Oh God, yes. Oh, my God." He gasped, hardly able to stand.

"Harry, please take your hat off." And she slid his bone-hard organ deep into her mouth.

7

The sheriff of Medicine Fork and environs had just lighted a fresh cigar. It was an especially good Havana, given him in congratulations at mounting an overwhelming vote. To be sure, nobody could have given even a vague explanation of what territory Slocum was sheriff of, or whether he might not in fact be a marshal and not a sheriff at all. These were fine points, of small moment. The point was that nobody—*nobody*—wanted a real lawman about. Slocum understood that. He understood the job was political, simply fancy clothing; and he was amused.

He drew on his cigar, enjoying the full aroma of the pale smoke as it rose toward the ceiling of the single-room shack that had been designated as the marshal's office. Not knowing what he was for sure, legally, people had already fallen into the habit of calling him "Marshal." It was all right with Slocum. It was quite all right with Marshal John Slocum, sheriff of "a certain amount of territory in and around a place called Medicine Fork." He reached up now and with his calloused thumb rubbed the tin star that was pinned to his hickory shirt.

He was sitting on an upended barrel facing two upended crates. On top of this makeshift table his Colt revolver lay disassembled on a piece of chamois. He had cleaned the whole gun carefully and charged the chambers. His .44-.40 Winchester and .50 Sharps rifles lay nearby on another upended crate. The rifles were covered with petroleum jelly. The jelly had a terrible smell to it, but it kept the weapons from rusting. Taking plenty of time, Slocum cleaned each rifle.

Then, as he had done with his handguns, he tested each weapon for balance. Finally, he worked on the cut-down shotgun. He really needed that weapon with the wide scatter. Nothing like a load of blue whistlers aimed right at a man's lynch pin to convince a mob that they were being indiscreet.

It was the lull now, he was thinking, as he put down the shotgun and drew pleasurably on his cigar. Well, good enough. He was as ready as he could be. Yet he felt the trace of unease gnawing at him.

Bruin hadn't been at the parade and he hadn't been about on the day of the election. Only his watchdog Chiverton had been in evidence. And keeping a wide berth from himself, Slocum was pleased to note.

In a sense, the election had been too easy. Bruin

hadn't lifted a finger. And from what Slocum knew of the man, this wasn't at all like him. Except he did have the reputation of being a fox.

He had heard that Bruin was hanging out in one of the box canyons at Bitter Hole and came to town rarely. Yes, the old buzzard had tossed the election away. And then too, why hadn't Bruin opposed Wilfong when the wagons had come in? What was he up to?

Well, there was nothing Slocum could do at the moment to force Bruin's hand, even if he'd wanted to. The best thing was to wait and watch. Meanwhile, there were the two wolfers. As lawman in the territory now, he could get up a posse and smoke them out. He was going to have to see Yellow Horse pretty soon. The Shoshone chief was patient, but how patient were his people? Slocum had promised to bring the two wolfers in, and he had better get them there before much more time passed.

He returned to the question: what was Harry Bruin up to? What did Bruin know about the railroad? Did he know something Spider didn't? Was that why he was playing it so easy?

The town was growing. Tents were raised, and tent houses, a combination of canvas and wood frame. Cabins were being built, some log, but most with old lumber. Spider had brought in a good amount of building materials. He seemed to have thought of just about everything, Slocum decided. Just about. Slocum had a nasty feeling that the little gambler had not taken into full account the caliber of the man he was dealing with. Harry Bruin wasn't some run-of-the-mill gambler, the win a few, lose a few kind who took his losses, got out of the game, and looked for what the next hand was going to be. But Spider wouldn't listen. He was riding high and tall.

More shacks were built to house the girls who, under the sharp surveillance of Cassie Wilfong, plied their wares with skill and profit. There were no complaints. The two saloons were doing a brisk business. There was a barber and bath, a blacksmith, a general store, two eateries, and a big tent where wayward travelers could rest, and even sleep. There were some smaller, individual tents which Spider—ever the enterprising opportunist—was renting as homes.

Slocum's duties were hardly onerous. A few drunks to corral, an occasional brawl, someone riding his horse fast through town or shooting off a gun —these were the lawbreakers. He watched the games at the two saloons like a hawk. He knew that sooner or later Spider was going to start rigging the odds for the house, and he was sure Cyrus at the Big Elk would do the same. For the moment, his nightly presence kept them honest. But he knew that when the last track was laid and the cowboys started coming in with the herds the town was going to bust wide open. He expected to be gone by then. By now he had decided simply to track down LeFranc and Lime and hand them over to Yellow Horse. And he was hoping at some point to make contact with Barclay. She still gave him the cold smile, the toothy greeting, and he was getting to the boiling point. There was something about her that even his roaring nights in bed with Cassie Wilfong couldn't ease. By golly, he told himself, he was as horny for that schoolmarm as any young kid. And if she could ever get her school going, maybe she'd settle down and try to be human. One day he decided to try a fresh approach.

"Miss Barclay, ma'am," he said, touching the brim of his hat as they met in the street one afternoon. "I'd surely like to take some lessons with you." And to her icy glare he added, "I see you don't have any pupils yet, there being hardly any families here, or kids."

"There are some, Mr. Slocum. Some who came on the wagon train, if you perhaps noticed. I'm teaching them in their homes for the moment."

"Until Chiverton sets you up, huh?" he said, wryly.

"I don't see that as being any of your business, sir."

She was starting to walk away with her nose up in the air. He thought she looked delightful. "Chiverton is my business, lady. I am warning you on that man. You had better watch him." He said it hard, putting plenty of meaning into his words. "You listen to me," he went on. "If you want to ignore John Slocum, all right. You take your chances there. That's social. But, by God, you get off your high horse when the law talks to you. I'm the law in this town, and I'm telling you to watch that man. Don't do something dumb that you'll regret."

He could tell that it really hit her. She walked away from him, her cheeks darkening. At the same time, as the moment lengthened he found his eyes had dropped to her lively haunches, and he could feel his erection almost splitting his trousers. Well, what could a man do with a hot little piece of ice like that? Cassie Wilfong really caught hell that night.

The railroad was moving steadily closer. The track layers were in sight, and already strangers were coming into town wanting to buy land and set up business; land and enterprises which Spider Wilfong mostly controlled. He was already talking with ranchers while cattle pens were being put up.

Yet, the more swiftly the town grew, the closer the railroad tracks came, the more Slocum felt the question rankling him: What was Harry Bruin up to? Yes, he controlled some of the real estate, but damn little, thanks to Spider Wilfong, and none of it on Main Street.

One day Slocum spotted Chiverton walking along the street. He was across the way from where Slocum was standing in conversation with Preacher Chimes, who had started Sunday services in one of the tents. Attendance was respectable, even good, and the Preacher was beaming. He had even married a young couple two days before, although Slocum wondered about the legality of the act since Chimes's clerical status was not really official, he suspected. Still, he gave the congregation what it wanted: bread and jam.

As he listened to Chimes telling him how wonderful it was to be in Medicine Fork, Slocum's eyes were on Chiverton, who had just stopped to talk to a grizzled old sourdough leading a burro loaded down with mining tools and equipment. He looked like any old prospector out of the hills.

On a hunch, he crossed the street and walked quickly up to Chiverton and the old sourdough to see if he could catch something of their conversation.

The old prospector had a gravelly voice that never seemed to leave the back of his throat. "And like I said, friend, I bin prospectin' these hills longer'n I care to remember and I have found just about enough silver to fill a hound's tooth."

"It's no El Dorado, eh?" said Slocum, ignoring Chiverton's scowl at his intrusion.

"No sir, it ain't."

"Were you here then? Were you here in Medicine Fork when the mines were going?"

"Silver City they called 'er then. Why, the stuff run like water." His eyes grew wild and his hands painted the air in front of him. "Why, I mind the ore wagons that . . ."

Suddenly he stopped and in a flash Slocum felt something come into the atmosphere. He felt it coming from Chiverton.

"Well," the old man went on. "No mining now. Just bits an' pieces I pick up around. Keeps body and soul in one piece. Sometimes. Sometimes," he added.

"Would you join me for a drink?" Slocum said.

Chiverton had pushed his way between them. "Slocum, you are interrupting a conversation here. Charlie and I are busy. Good day to you."

Slocum grinned. "Don't bust a ball over it, sonny." He turned to Charlie. "See ya."

He stood watching them making their way down to the Big Elk. The old man, Charlie, tied his burro to the hitch rail and then followed Chiverton into the tent.

Slocum had an impulse to get down there and examine what the burro was packing, but he refrained. It would be a big mistake if Chiverton or any of his boys happened to see him examining the old prospector's gear.

He stood there listening to the not-so-distant wail of a locomotive punching slowly down to the end-of-track. It sounded mournful to him, and he wondered why. He wondered how it sounded to the Indians.

Then he snapped out of his reverie. There was no time for that. The whistle had called him to dream, but now when it sounded again it was calling him to action. It wouldn't be long now before things had to come to a head. Not long at all. And he had better be ready.

He found Spider Wilfong in his wagon sitting cross-legged on his bedding practicing with a shaved deck of cards. Dressed only in his long-handled underwear and his big Stetson hat, the little man was surrounded by his advantage tools, the equipment with which he plied his trade: a holdout which could be placed under the sleeve of his coat and attached to his shoulder, from which a card could be dropped into his palm, or into which a card could "disappear;" the blue tinted glasses that could read marked cards where the naked eye was unable; the dice that had been topped and only threw combinations of seven or, on the other hand, never threw it.

"Come in, my friend. Man has to keep his hand in or he gets rusty. That way with the gun hawks, ain't it?" He put down his deck of shaved cards, picked up a regular deck, and began dealing seconds.

"What's Bruin up to?" Slocum asked. "You know him."

"Hah!" Spider swiftly dealt a round of poker to four mythical players, his lips moving, totally concentrated. When he was done, he cocked a shrewd eye at Slocum. "It'll be a full house you've got there, my friend." And he pointed.

Slocum turned the cards over. "Not bad."

Phineas P. Wilfong snorted in indignation. "Not bad! It's goddamn good!"

He sniffed and reached for his cigar butt, which

had been lying cold and dead on the bed near his hand.

"I know Bruin, yes," he said. "But then I don't know him."

"He's awful quiet. What does he know about the railroad?"

"He knows they're coming. Hell, we can all hear 'em down track. But he may or may not know when." Spider sniffed. "He knows I got the land grants and property papers here for the best spots in town. Since I won 'em."

"What do you figure Bruin's really up to?"

"I hear something extra in what you're saying."

"I'm saying Bruin hasn't lifted a finger to stop you. How come?"

"I got him buffaloed."

"In a pig's eye! He's playing his cards real close."

In the pause that followed, Spider Wilfong sniffed. "What you figger, huh?"

"I figure there's two ways he can go," Slocum said. "As of this moment."

"Such as?"

"Such as he can try to bust the town, wipe you out, and just take over by force."

"I've thought of that. What else?"

"The other is get the railroad to finish their track laying someplace else."

Spider's rubbery lips pursed and his eyes grew big and round. "Interesting choice," he said. "What you reckon he'll do?"

"Both."

"Both!"

"You're a gambler, Spider; don't you always keep at least a pair of options going?" He stood up, bending slightly due to his height.

"Where you off to?" the gambler asked as Slocum moved toward the front of the wagon.

"Figure I'll take a look at some of those options. He could have more than two, I do believe."

The little spotted horse picked his way down the narrow switchback trail that Slocum had discovered up at the rim. When they were about halfway down into the box canyon he drew up to give some study to how he would proceed. He was still pretty high up, and he could just see a corner of the log cabin's sod roof below.

It was mid-afternoon but the sun would set early here in the high land, and he was eager to get down to the cabin and scout around before it got dark. Dismounting, he led the horse to a stand of spruce near an overhanging rock. They were well protected; he was sure that Harry Bruin would have outriders guarding any entrance to the box canyon. And so he had moved with extra caution.

The ledge was too prominent for his sighting into the canyon; he could be spotted too easily. He moved to the edge of the trees, took the field glasses out of his possibles bag, and finding new cover he focused on the log cabin directly below. It looked like an old miner's or trapper's soddy, solid as any fort against Indian attack, army assault, or the weather—not to mention the law.

He had made sure that no sunlight reflected off the glasses that would give him away. Easiest mistake in the world, but like so many mistakes in this country, you only made it once. After a few moments he changed his position for a clearer view, which he

found through a narrow opening in the pines below.
He could see the whole of the log house. Two other
cabins were also in view, both with sod roofs and
both in need of repair. He wondered if he was looking at the hideout of the old Bitter Hole gang. Very
likely, he reasoned, since Harry Bruin had chosen
this particular spot for his headquarters. It had the
advantage of his familiarity with the country plus the
network of box canyons all through the area that
would confuse any intruder. The canyon below, like
most box canyons, apparently had only one entrance,
which was also the exit. Yet he knew that there had
to be another way into and out of the canyon; no
outlaw in his right mind would set himself up with no
way out like that. He had spent the better part of the
morning finding the game trail over the rimrocks. So
there was at least one way in and out other than the
obvious entrance through the high slabs of stone. If
this had been a hideout for Bruin's old Bitter Hole
gang, it was a damn good one.

From one of the cabins a pale pencil of smoke
rose skyward. Probably the bunkhouse, he reasoned,
wondering how many men Bruin would have with
him. He could also see the round horse corral just
beyond the second cabin. There were three horses,
one of them licking at a salt block in the center of the
corral, the other two standing close together and now
and again shaking off flies.

Three, with one of them likely Bruin's. Still, he
wasn't satisfied. Why would that old slicker be out
here with only two men? There must be others
outriding—sentries. Say there were half a dozen
here; would LeFranc and Lime be among them?

He crawled back to his horse and slipped the glasses into his bag. Then, lifting the thong off his six-shooter, he started on foot down the narrow, bony trail, which had sufficient cover to keep him out of sight of anyone below as long as he was careful.

In another fifteen minutes he was down on a level with the corral and its three horses. Off to the right he saw the barn, a log structure with a second corral connected to it so that a horse could come from the barn out into the corral by itself, and return. There was still no sign of any men, only the slow, vague smoke coming out of the second cabin.

But somehow he wasn't satisfied. And it occurred to him that maybe this wasn't Bruin's place at all. Now, slipping around the corral to the other side of the two cabins, he saw the trail leading farther down and across from the ranch. In a jiffy he had worked his way down and had started to ease along through scrub oak and high bunch grass.

A shift on the wind brought the strong smell of horses, and then suddenly he was at the clearing. Before him was another cabin and a big rope corral in which he counted nearly forty head. Even counting a change of mount, say two head per man, it meant that Bruin had a band of at least twenty to a couple of dozen men. Twenty men meant twenty guns; and, realizing the caliber of Harry Bruin, he knew the caliber of his men, and the strength of their firepower.

What was the man planning to do, ride in and take over Medicine Fork at gunpoint? With a cadre like that he could do it. It explained why he hadn't fought the election. And what was more, the horseflesh was the best, Slocum noted. A top outlaw would be bound to ride only the best. After all, it was a matter of healthy business.

He was still reflecting on what Harry Bruin was up to when he heard the door of the cabin open and someone swearing casually. Quickly he ducked behind some bullberry bushes.

"Looks like he's getting ready directly now," a voice said.

"Yeah? Ready for what?" He recognized the voice of Felix LeFranc.

"Dunno," said the first man.

Was it Lime? Peering out, he saw their backs. Yes, LeFranc. There was no mistaking the broad back and greasy, slouching walk. But it was not Jake Lime with him. Somebody Slocum had never seen before.

But he wanted LeFranc and Lime together. Taking one, even if he could do so, would only alert the other and make it that much more difficult to catch him.

He waited while the voices faded as the men walked past the big open horse corral.

Listening carefully, he could hear nothing out of the ordinary. It was cooling now as the sun moved closer to the horizon. Already there were lengthening shadows on the land. Quickly he moved away from his hiding place, heading through the trees toward the first cabin, the one he had taken to be Bruin's. In a few moments he reached a stand of box elders that afforded him protection while he could look directly onto the aged log house. While he had been down watching the horses and listening to LeFranc and his companion, a gig had driven up to Bruin's cabin. Its passengers had evidently gone inside. The animal standing patiently between the shafts was a sleek sorrel mare with a wide white blaze on her forehead. It didn't look like an outfit someone had rented from the livery in Medicine Fork. A pretty fancy rig and a sound horse like that spoke for a man of substance, someone from out of the country.

Suddenly the door opened and a heavyset man of maybe fifty came out, followed by Clay Chiverton, with an older gray-headed man wearing a handgun low on his hip bringing up the rear, and not bothering to close the door. It could only be Harry Bruin, Slocum noted, appreciating the way Bruin let his visitors go out before him, also just in case. As the three walked toward the gig, Chiverton and the other man talking, Slocum kept his eyes closely on Bruin. The man moved smoothly, and with full alertness. His eyes were everywhere, missing nothing. He even looked directly at Slocum at one point, but surely couldn't see through the thick foliage. Even so, Slocum's hand had dropped to his sixgun.

The visitor had reached the gig and now he turned back to Chiverton and Bruin. Slocum could hear his words clearly.

"Well, Mr. Bruin, I think we are pretty well in accord."

Harry Bruin was watching Chiverton as he held out a hand to help the visitor step up into the gig and then climbed up himself.

Bruin didn't speak right away. Instead he turned his head to one side and spat sparingly in the direction of the sorrel mare. "Nice-lookin' piece of horse-flesh you got there, Soames."

"I appreciate a good horse, Mr. Bruin."

Chiverton chuckled, lifting the reins. "The company takes care of its important men, the men it relies on," he said amiably.

"Let's let it take care of yours truly then," replied Bruin, his voice deep with intention. With a nod toward the man named Soames, and ignoring Chiverton, he turned on his heel and started back to the cabin.

Chiverton slapped the reins lightly on the sorrel's back and the gig took off, with his companion holding onto his thin hat.

Slocum was watching Harry Bruin, who had turned as he reached the cabin door. For a moment he stood in the open doorway with his thumbs hooked into his gunbelt, looking after the departing gig from beneath the low brim of his hat. Then he spat, turned, and walked into the cabin, closing the door behind him.

The sky was fading fast as Slocum made his way back up to where he had left his horse. Looking to the east he saw a single star, bright in the swiftly darkening sky.

It was slow going leading the spotted horse back up the thin, hard trail, and it took longer than he wished. By the time they had reached the top of the rimrocks and crossed over and down the other side to the main trail, it was halfway through the night. Satisfied that he wasn't followed he pulled into a little hollow alongside a creek and here he made camp. He picketed the horse close by, drew his Colt, and, lying down fully clothed, slept with the gun in his hand.

In the morning he awakened with the first suggestion of light, looking across at a coyote, who was less than fifty feet away and watching him.

He would have given a lot for some hot coffee, but it was no time to build a fire. Bruin could easily have outriders who would spot the smoke. After chewing some hardtack and washing it down with creek water, he mounted the spotted horse and headed toward Medicine Fork. He moved slowly, walking the horse and keeping under cover whenever possible, checking his back trail and whatever part of the country came into his vision. It was dicey. When he moved down to the lower country he found he was exposed to anyone who should happen onto the ridge he had left. It was dangerous, but there was nothing he could do about it except keep going. From time to time he scanned the ridge, fearful of becoming a wide-open target.

He was careful all the way down the long sweep of land that ran from the edge of the trees like rushing water, ending in a long valley, where he startled some deer who had been grazing peacefully.

He crossed a narrow valley and on the other side he rode through a big stand of pine. Just before coming out into the open again he drew rein. Again he sat his horse in the shadow of the trees, scouting the country ahead before making a move, looking to see how the shadows fell, how the birds flew. He felt uneasy. Something was bothering him, and he wasn't sure what it was.

During the night he had heard thunder and seen lightning, but it hadn't actually rained where he had camped. Here it had. The ground was still damp, even soaked in some places, and some of the rocks, though drying, were still slippery. The land, the air, even the light shared the new freshness. And he still felt uneasy.

He was about to move on in spite of his uneasiness when he saw the three riders come from under the trees on the highest part of the ridge opposite. From where they were they had a clear view of the area where he sat his horse, but fortunately he was well back in the shadow of the trees and, he hoped, invisible to them as long as he remained still.

Slocum drew the pony back, turning him. He'd have to find another way. After a few moments' search he found a kind of trail, made by game probably, leading in the direction he wanted to go. It would take longer, but it was safer than going out into the open while those three riders were about.

He walked the horse, weaving in and out through the spruce, pine, and fir. Finally the trail widened. Slocum drew up again, listening. There was only the sound of the trees moving with the slight breeze.

He nudged the pony with his knee, clucked once with his tongue, heading west toward the town. The trees began to thin and he knew that soon he would have a view all the way to Medicine Fork.

He had been riding another hour or more when he suddenly felt the uneasiness. Instantly his inner warning voice sounded. Without an instant's hesitation he turned the pony and scrambled up a rise of ground into a thick stand of spruce, and began weaving through the dense trees and around deadfalls, of which there were many, into denser cover. Finally he pulled up and waited.

After a moment he heard something. A rider was approaching. More than one. They were close, and now he even saw something moving through the trees.

They were two and they were following his

tracks. In a moment they'd find the place where he
and his horse had left the trail and gone up the rise
into the thicker trees.

Taking a quick look, he saw a thin opening where
it was possible to go. Looking back, he saw that the
pair of horsemen had drawn rein and were listening.
Both were in line for a clear shot. He had already
unlooped the thong from the hammer of his handgun.

"Hold it right there!" Slocum's voice startled
them. Perhaps they hadn't thought he was that close.

The rider who was to his left jerked around,
bringing up his pistol. Slocum fired. The man was
hardly forty feet away, but his horse spooked even
before the shot and Slocum's bullet, aimed at the
man's chest, grazed his neck. Not at all fatal, but it
was enough to frighten him.

Slocum kicked his pony deeper into the trees,
weaving through the timber and starting into a run as
they hit the further edge of the trees and came out
into a small meadow.

"Get the son of a bitch!" one of the men yelled.

"The sonofabitch got me!" The voice was filled
with pain, anger, and something like defeat.

Nevertheless, both riders were coming on. Slocum broke around a thick stand of bullberry bush.
Yanking the Winchester out of its scabbard, he
dropped off his horse, who pulled up after running a
few feet. Slocum was running as he hit the ground,
disappearing into thick cover fast. Abruptly he
stopped so as not to make noise that would give him
away. With the Winchester at the ready he waited.

They were talking as they dismounted and started
toward the bushes, spread out, not making a single
target. And then suddenly he saw them in the clear:
LeFranc and Lime. In the same instant he saw their

horses, recognizing them from when they had been on the high ridge across from him earlier.

In that same flash of recognition, the alarm rang through him, and just in time. He heard the branch snap behind him and he ducked, rolled, dropping the Winchester, and came up with the Colt, coughing out three shots and watching the third man drop.

Without more than a snap glance to see that he was dead, he spun back, snatched up the Winchester, and fired, knocking the rifle out of Jake Lime's hand.

"Right now!" The words snapped out harder than bullets. The two men froze. "Drop your guns, and unbuckle!"

When he stepped out from the bushes he caught the surprise on their faces.

"Yep, it's me, boys. Slocum."

"Too bad," LeFranc said. "We thought it was somebody else." He was staring at the star on Slocum's shirt. "Got yerself a piece of tin, huh."

"That's right. You boys are through."

"Gonna throw us into jail? What for?" Lime said.

"Why, I'm not going to throw you into jail."

"Probably try to drygulch us someplace," Felix said.

"Not that either, boys. Get your horses."

"What about him?" LeFranc said, looking past Slocum.

"He is dead. You want to pack him along, do you?"

"He is talking about me, Mr. Slocum, not the unfortunate Zeke." Clay Chiverton stepped out of the underbrush to his left, followed by a half dozen men, fanning out around the clearing. "And I am definitely not dead. And neither are my companions."

8

They had tied his hands behind him and one of the men had taken the reins of his horse and was leading him. It was not an easy ride, not with his hands so tightly bound in back of him. Chiverton was in a hurry, besides. LeFranc and Lime rode close to Slocum, looking at him, passing remarks.

"Lucky thing we got our orders," LeFranc said, cocking an eye toward their prisoner but speaking to Jake Lime. "Otherwise . . ." He let it hang.

Lime finished it. "Otherwise we'd pay him back for that time he hit you when you weren't looking. Same like he done to Harry Bruin's kid brother, so I hear."

Slocum said nothing.

Felix LeFranc had been chewing a big clump of tobacco. Now he leaned over and dropped a load of brown and yellow saliva mixed with small pieces of tobacco. Lifting his head, he let fly a stream just off his horse's withers. He sniffed. "Fucking bastard." He looked over at Slocum, who was ignoring him. "Had his eye set for that schoolmarm, by God."

"You noticed it, eh?" laughed Lime.

"Nice woman there. You ever get to try her out, Slocum?"

LeFranc's little eyes squeezed tighter with laughter.

"Watch that dirty mouth, mister!" Chiverton, riding up, had overheard. "You don't talk about a lady in that way with this—this man!" He nodded toward the prisoner. "And you, you'll be in a place where you can keep your filthy thoughts to yourself in respect to your betters."

"Jealous, huh?" Slocum grinned at the dapper Chiverton, sitting like a board on his big chestnut horse.

"Mind your mouth, mister!" Chiverton kicked his horse right up alongside Slocum and suddenly slapped him with the back of his hand, right across the mouth.

"I see you haven't lost your courage, you son of a bitch!"

Chiverton's hand had dropped to his chest.

"Going to pull your hideout on me?" Slocum asked, licking the corner of his mouth, from which blood was trickling.

"There'll be time," Chiverton snapped. "I promise you that, Slocum. You will be paid in full."

"Why don't we dump the son of a bitch right

now?" Lime asked. "Looks to me like we can all of us settle up and be shut of him."

"Mr. Bruin wants to see him," Chiverton said, holding his burning eyes on Slocum. His grin was like a knife across his thin face.

"Everybody loves the bastard," sneered Felix. He cut his horse viciously across the rump as he shied at something along the trail.

It was at the hottest part of the day when they stopped to water the horses.

"Got to take a leak," Slocum said. "You better untie my hands."

"Got a mind not to," Jake Lime mumbled when Chiverton nodded.

"You try anything funny I'll cut yer balls off," Lime said.

"I'll still have more balls than you," Slocum said, and for his trouble he received a smash in the kidney from the barrel of Lime's handgun.

When they were mounted up again, his main regret was that he had promised them to Yellow Horse. He wondered if maybe he could make a deal with the chief, but then knew it was an idle thought. It was not a deal situation as far as the Shoshone chief was concerned.

For the rest of the time he occupied himself with how he could make a break for it. But there was no opportunity; not with his hands tied behind his back, his guns taken, and with three dedicated enemies riding almost as close to him as his skin; not to mention the half dozen other riders who made up the group.

In a while they reached the box canyon. It was one of many, with extremely high walls and a narrow, almost invisible entrance. These canyons made a natural corral, especially useful for stolen stock, as the outlaws well knew.

Bitter Hole, like most of its kind of canyon had only one entrance—and the same exit—as far as anyone knew. And it was through this entrance they now rode, a narrow trail between high slabs of vertical rock. Slocum, thinking of the other trail which he had discovered and used already, wondered if there might be yet a third place of entry, one through which stock might be run. It was a half-formed thought and it gave way to his surprise on seeing Charlie the prospector and his burro just outside of Harry Bruin's cabin.

They rode right on by the cabin to the trees that opened out onto the big rope corral in the clearing. There were more horses there now, Slocum saw, and some men were lounging around the steps of what he took to be the bunkhouse.

The riders began to peel off as they crossed the clearing along the outside of the rope corral, going single file, with Chiverton and the two wolfers sticking right with him. Presently they reached a cutbank and reined their horses in front of a big heavy door with a padlock on it.

All of them dismounted save for Chiverton, who sat his chestnut, watching. LeFranc took a big key out of his pocket and opened the padlock and pushed the door. It moved open with difficulty for the earth had filled around its frame and it was slightly askew.

"Inside," Chiverton said, looking down from his horse.

The two wolfers took Slocum's arms and shoved him into the room.

Inside it was pitch dark. He had the feeling it must

be an abandoned root cellar.

"How about cutting my hands free?" he said. "Are you afraid I'll get out?"

"Cut him free," Chiverton said. "He isn't going anywhere."

Lime did the trick, not without taking a little nick in his prisoner's wrist.

The door slammed behind him and he heard the padlock snap home.

The darkness was total. He stood quite still, smelling the dampness, the earth. Luckily he had matches. He struck one and took a quick look around. It was a fairly large room, obviously cut into the bank, for the walls were of earth and so was the floor. There was a broken-down table, a battered chair, some old blankets on one side of the room. No window, of course, but there was a lamp and it had coal oil in it. He struck another match and lighted it.

Swiftly, but with care, he inspected his surroundings. A more or less typical root cellar. Only there was no food in the random jars that lay about the few shelves that had not fallen down. He especially examined the wall in which the door was cut, in the hope that he might be able to dig his way out. But it was far too thick, and solidly packed, and of course he had no tools. He heard a sound then and saw a huge pack rat race across the floor and into a hole in the corner of the cellar. Well, he reflected dryly, he wouldn't want for company.

He sat down at the table now, and lowered the lamp wick as far as he could to conserve oil. What were they planning to do with him? He rose and again made an inspection of the room, but closer this time, looking for even the slightest opening, for any article that might be used as a weapon. Nothing. Not a thing. The room was impregnable. But now, to his surprise, he realized that there was a door in the far corner that he hadn't noticed. There was no knob, no lock; it was simply sealed shut, with the earth caked in around its frame. It was absolutely immovable.

He sat down again, killing the light for fear of running out of oil. He sat for a long time in total darkness, thinking on his situation, and how he could get away.

How long he sat there he had no idea, but he must have dozed off, for the next thing he realized there was a sound at the door. He half rose from his seat as the door swung open and a lantern lighted the room. Obviously it was dark outside. How long had he been here? He didn't worry about that; his attention was on the figure who entered.

"Don't be foolish," the woman said. "Don't try to make a break for it. Felix is out there with a sawed-off shotgun."

She was carrying a tray of food along with the storm lantern. Crossing to the table, she put it down. Then she returned to the door and shut it firmly. Turning to face him, she brushed her blond hair out of her eyes.

Slocum saw that she was young, not more than thirty, he would have sworn. And she was quite lovely. Her eyes were widely spaced, and she had a short, turned-up nose. Beneath her mass of blond hair he could just see the lobes of each ear. She stood quite still as he looked her up and down, his eyes resting on her bosom, which was high, firm, and altogether provocative.

"Well, I do hope you find the goods satisfactory,

Mr. Slocum." Her tone was neutral, and he couldn't quite tell whether she was teasing him or not. "Would you like some supper?"

"I would if you'll join me."

"You eat," she said, picking up a crate and bringing it over to the table to use as a seat, "and this time I'll do the looking."

"Dumb! Dumb an' stupid, puttin' him in that root cellar! What the hell's the matter with you?"

Harry Bruin stood glaring at his "pupil" across the table on which was a bottle of whiskey and a single glass, half filled—Harry's.

"It was the safest place," Clay Chiverton insisted. "He can't possibly get out of there. And, anyway, I've got a guard with a cut-down Greener waiting for him if he does."

"He can't get out of anywhere, you dumb shit, if you've got a halfway decent guard on him. A couple of guards," Bruin added quickly, reaching for his glass.

"Well, where else? You want us to chain him outside?" Chiverton scratched the back of his neck. He was prone to boils, had been since childhood, and now he had a new one growing. "Or in the barn?" Suddenly he looked curiously at Bruin. "Why not the root cellar? Why not? It isn't being used for anything."

Bruin didn't answer. He reached for the bottle, sloshed whiskey into his thick, scarred tumbler, and took a good swig.

"Aah!" He smacked his lips in pleasure. "More like it, that is!" His grim look softened. "No. Leave him there. Hah!" He rubbed his nose with his thumb knuckle. "With the rats. I'll talk to him in the morning."

"You want him worked over some?" Chiverton asked, and the old outlaw caught the eagerness in his voice.

"Who? Yourself? Hah!" The snort of contempt seemed to bounce off the cabin walls, and he regarded the younger man with loaded eyes. "You work over Slocum? Holy shit! What are you trying to tell me?" A great roar of laughter burst out of him. It didn't just come from his open mouth, it came from his whole body, like a dam breaking. His entire body shook. Tears sprang to his eyes and poured down his creased cheeks. He crashed into the back of his chair, almost breaking it, but not even noticing, the power of his mirth was so great. Weak as a puppy, he almost fell to the floor, his shoulders shaking as he laughed, snorted, roared, belched, and finally collided with an upsurge of coughing, loose phlegm almost strangling him as he tried to cough and laugh at the same time.

Clay Chiverton sat glaring furiously in molten embarrassment at this man he truly hated.

Again, the old man all but fell right out of his chair. He recovered, straightened up, and took a drink, wiping his streaming eyes and dripping nose with a huge red bandanna.

To silence him, if indeed that were possible, Chiverton began again to speak. "What do you plan to do with him? Are we going to hold him out here while we ride in and take the town?" He made a sudden face as the boil on the back of his neck stabbed him. "Why not just shoot him and dump him in a gulch somewhere?"

"What's the hurry? Lesson number two hundred

and fifty-four: make use of everything and everybody. When—*if*—we find we can't find a way to use him, then we'll dump him."

"I'd like to handle that," Chiverton said.

"I just bet you would." Bruin looked slyly at the man seated across from him. "I just bet you would. But do not forget lesson number one."

Chiverton waited. He knew Bruin wanted him to ask what that was, but he refused, he absolutely refused. His anger had swept beyond prudence, and even though he knew this he didn't care.

Harry Bruin sat watching him, grinning and drinking, lifting the glass and lowering it. His pale blue eyes never left Chiverton's face.

It was an endless moment, and then Chiverton said, "Which is?"

"Which is—what?"

Chiverton wanted to scream. He said, "What is lesson number one?"

Harry Bruin's nose twitched. He remembered something from many years back, from his childhood; somebody, maybe his mother, telling him that when your nose itched it meant someone was going to kiss you. The thought slipped in, swift as silk, and then out. Gone. He was wondering where Annie was.

"Lesson number one," he said, "is that you don't do nothing without me—*me*—telling you." He rubbed his nose with the back of his hand. "Telling you who, when, where, and how."

He was looking right into his pupil's eyes. "You got it?"

Clay Chiverton nodded. He dropped his eyes. "Got it."

• • •

"Are you going to watch me eat?" Slocum said as she sat down at the opposite side of the table.

"Do you mind?"

"Want to join me?"

"I've already eaten." She was wearing a shawl and now she swept it back and brought out a bottle of whiskey.

"Now that's more like it," he said with a grin.

"I'll join you with this," she said. She brought a second glass out of somewhere; he didn't bother to notice. She was damn good-looking. Her hair was silky like corn, and her eyes were very blue. She had a full, wide mouth, delicious.

"Do you have a name?"

"Annie."

"You're part of the establishment here?"

"I'm Harry Bruin's. Just for your information."

"I don't mind if you're Harry's."

"Thanks."

"He's got good taste, I see."

"Thanks again."

"You're welcome."

He had eaten all he wanted, not feeling very hungry, and now he leaned back and took a good pull at his whiskey. "You got any idea what they're keeping me for? They're messing with the law, you know."

Her eyes dropped to the tin star. "But you were trespassing. That's against the law."

"Not when you're an officer of the law."

"I don't believe that's how Harry looks at it."

Slocum reached to his shirt pocket, took out a quirly, and lighted it.

"Can I have one?" Her eyes danced at him, and

her mouth was not quite twitching.

"Sure." He handed her one, then struck a match for her.

She drew on the quirly with pleasure, her eyes still on him.

"So you were sent to spy on me, or to try to pump me. That it?"

"Maybe." Her smile broadened; her eyes were now on his lips.

"Did Harry tell you how far to go?"

"How far?" She seemed puzzled.

"What does he want to know?"

"I don't know."

"What do you want to know?" Slocum persisted. "Let me put it that way."

She raised her eyes now to look directly into his. There was a patch of color on each of her cheeks. Her lips were slightly apart, and now her eyes dropped again to his mouth. He didn't even attempt to remove his eyes from the swell of her breasts as she leaned against the edge of the table. His erection was charging at his trousers.

"What do I want to know?" she asked.

"That's what I said."

She leaned forward even more, and her eyes seemed to grow wider. "I want to know how big it is. That's what I want to know."

"I know of a good way to find out," he said, standing up and unbuckling his belt.

She was already pulling down her clothes, and his hands were on her taut, high breasts. He squeezed them, ran his fingers around the nipples and then took one of them in his mouth.

He entered her from the side and then she was on

top of him, riding him and crying with delight.

In the next moment he had turned her, without missing a stroke, and she was on her back, her legs drawn up high. They grabbed each other in a bear hug and in this way rode in perfect unison. He held off, driving her to the absolute pitch of mania, until at last he could stand it no longer and in a long, long moment their bucking loins thrashed the bedding halfway around the room.

They lay with their limbs entwined, exhausted.

When she was gone he got up and pulled on his pants and shoes, then carried the lamp over to the door in the back of the cellar. He had considered asking Annie where the door led, why it was sealed, but had changed his mind, not wanting to arouse suspicion on her part. He hadn't even glanced in that direction while she was there.

But now he remembered that there was something he had thought he'd noticed before. Bending close, he again saw the scratches in the dirt that had caked around the knob. Holding the lamp very close, he inspected the jamb, and realized that the door had been opened recently. No question. The earth had been jammed back into place to make it look as though nothing had disturbed it. But it had definitely been opened.

He stood back, puzzling the problem. What was in there? Where did it lead? Certainly it wasn't a way out. Or was it? Was there maybe a cache hidden there? Old outlaw loot? As far as he could recollect about the layout of the cutbank in which the root cellar was dug, the door couldn't possibly lead to any outside. It had to be another room, or some kind of cupboard. He stepped forward again and inspected the lock. It was an old lock, solid, and there would be no way of opening it without a key or some heavy tools.

Thwarted at least for the moment, he returned to his bed and lay down. He lay there in the dark feeling the dampness in his body, wondering what old Charlie the prospector had been doing out at Harry Bruin's cabin.

It wasn't long before he again heard someone at the root-cellar door. Almost immediately it was pushed open and daylight sprang through the doorway into the pitch-dark room. Before he even saw anyone he heard the gravelly voice.

"Just wanted to take a look at the son of a bitch who shot up my kid brother and thinks he got away with it."

Felix LeFranc was the first to enter, carrying his sixgun with his finger on the trigger. He was followed by Chiverton, looking hollow-eyed and tense, and finally the man who had to be the speaker with the gravelly voice, the man who could be no other than Harry Bruin. The old bandit looked indeed as though he had grown out of a gravel pit. Tough, knobby, he clearly didn't give an inch to the world.

Slocum remained as he was, lying on his back, gazing casually at the three men. His hands were at his sides, lying loose, yet ready to give him a push to his feet on an instant's notice.

He caught the sly look on Chiverton's face, and he didn't like it. Bruin's face, on the other hand, was impassive. The man was quiet, even stony, as he said, "Slocum..." Then he stopped and, without turning toward Felix LeFranc, he said, "Wait outside. Shut the door."

"Better light the lamp," Chiverton interrupted.

Bruin said nothing, only clearing his throat and
spitting hard onto the dirt floor. He waited while
Chiverton lighted the lamp and the wolfer departed.
Then he turned his attention back to the prisoner.

"I want some information, Slocum."

Slocum waited a moment and then slowly sat up,
swinging his legs around so that he sat crosslegged
on the blankets, his hands on his knees. He said
nothing, but kept his eyes on Bruin.

"I want you to tell me how much property Wilfong has got sewed up, how many cattlemen have
promised him they'll ship, and how many men and
guns he's got."

Slocum shifted his weight just a little, still not
answering right away. There was something wrong,
he knew. It just couldn't be these particular questions
that had caused Bruin to have him captured. He was
obviously after something else.

"I think you better ask Spider that," he said dryly.
Shifting his weight smoothly, he got quickly to his
feet and stood facing Bruin and Chiverton. "After
all, Harry, aren't you an old poker buddy of his?"

He watched the color flick darkly into the old outlaw's face as the taunt struck home.

Bruin's laugh was hard and scrabbly as he said,
"We could beat it out of you, Slocum."

"No you couldn't."

"I'd give you odds, mister."

"If the Sioux couldn't do it in three tries, you sure
can't."

Bruin's forehead wrinkled and his lips parted, re-
vealing brown teeth. "Stubborn bugger." He said it
more to himself than to either Slocum or Chiverton.

"What's it you really got a hard-on about, Bruin?"

A tight smile entered Bruin's eyes and touched the corner of his mouth as he pressed his cracked lips together. Slocum realized that he was whistling a little ditty to himself as he stood there facing him. It was hardly audible in the thick quiet of the root cellar.

"Chiverton . . ."

Clay Chiverton had taken out his jackknife and was cleaning his nails. He snapped the knife shut and looked toward Bruin.

"Perhaps seeing your friend might change his mind. Let's let him have a look."

To Slocum's surprise, Chiverton reddened. Clearly, whatever the plan was, he wasn't wholly in agreement. But it was also clear that he wasn't the man to argue with Bruin. He nodded.

Harry Bruin grinned, sticking the tip of his tongue out between his teeth. "Good enough."

Turning to Slocum, he said, "Tell you what we're gonna do, my friend. We're going to pay you back a debt. Know what I mean? I know you ain't the kind likes to owe anybody, so we're gonna wipe it all clean." His grin broadened. A thick cough suddenly hit him and he had to take a moment or two to clear it out. "I don't have a hard-on about anything, Slocum, my friend. Just want to clear up a little debt. I know you're going to be glad to do it. And . . ." He moved his hand in a calming gesture. "And you're right. It don't have nothing really to do with Spider. Old Spider . . ." He released a rich chuckle, his eyes never leaving Slocum's face. "Well, not all that much, anyways," he amended.

"Nice to know Spider's clean, leastways," Slocum said dryly.

Harry Bruin was grinning so broadly he was almost laughing. Slocum regarded him with his best poker face. He knew full well that that was what it was—another game of jacks or better. But with pretty stiff stakes, that was for sure.

"There's a Miss Barclay. Laurie?" Bruin cut his eye quickly to Chiverton.

"Loretta," Chiverton said.

Slocum felt something knife through his insides.

"I do believe you know the lady," Harry Bruin was saying. "Chiverton here, and also Felix and Lime, tell me as how you have got eyes for the lady."

"Is that your business, mister?"

"Chiverton tells me she wants to start a school in Medicine Fork, and he's promised to help her, by God. She is coming out to the canyon this evening to talk it over. You're bringing her, ain't you?" He turned to Chiverton, and then looked back at Slocum, letting his words hang in the air.

"You have got to be pretty hard up, Bruin, pretty used up to try pulling something like that."

"I'm not thinking of pulling anything, Slocum. It's you. It's yourself just thought of that. Ain't it so?"

"I am warning you, Bruin, you try any monkey shit with someone like that, the whole country'll be after your neck, and by God they'll stretch it all the way."

Harry Bruin's grin was really wicked now. "But no. No, my friend. It won't be me that gets his neck stretched. It'll be you. It'll be Slocum. Easy enough to pin anything that happens to that sweet innocent woman on Slocum. Slocum, the ladies' man." He was smiling all over now, nodding in rich agreement with himself.

Then he resumed. "She'll be here 'fore sundown, late afternoon time, on account of she's figuring on getting back to town before dark. The boys will bring you out for a look-see, just so you surely see Harry Bruin is not funnin' you."

Slocum felt it swimming inside him. Had Bruin gone crazy? Would he really go that far? Surely not just to know Spider's business! But why, then? To set up something like that was the work of a really crazy mind. No wonder Chiverton was looking so uneasy.

"You'll never get away with it, Harry."

"I'm not trying to get away with anything, mister. It's you who'll never get away with it."

Bruin had taken out a wooden match and was picking his teeth. "And even so, that sweet little gal; I mean, if she's all that pretty—and Chiverton here tells me she truly is—then she might be all that handy for a handsome feller like yours truly. Huh?" He was laughing all over his knotty face.

"Jesus . . ."

"That man has got nothing to do with this," Bruin said, and burst into a shout of laughter.

Then Slocum found an idea. "How is Annie going to handle it, then?" he said, drilling the words right into the laughing outlaw.

The big laugh froze right on Bruin's face, and from ruddy good humor he turned dark with anger. "You watch yer fuckin' mouth, Slocum! What d'you know! What d'you know about Annie, by God!"

"I know she's a real hot lay. I mean, for a handsome young feller like me."

For an instant, rage seemed to paralyze Bruin, but that passed and swift as a whisper he had his big sixgun out. But instead of firing, he slammed it against Slocum's arm. Chiverton had his gun out covering as Slocum staggered.

The pain burned through him, while the second slash with the big gun lay into the side of his neck, and as he felt himself going down, Bruin hit him in the head.

Harry Bruin holstered his sixgun. He looked at Chiverton, who was still pointing his derringer at the prone Slocum.

"You're learning, boy." And he nodded.

"Can't we just finish him off?"

Bruin was shaking his head.

"But why involve the girl?"

Bruin looked at him. "You're soft as baby shit, for Christ's sake. But calm yourself, we're not going to do anything to the girl."

"But what was all that you were telling him? I don't get it."

"We're not going to do anything. Someone... maybe Felix and Lime, they can rough her up a bit. In the dark so she don't know who it is."

"And then we spread the story that it was Slocum."

"Go to the top of the class!" His teacher was beaming.

"But why? Why not just kill the son of a bitch and be shut of him?"

Harry was again shaking his head, and more vigorously this time, as he warmed to the picture he was seeing in his thoughts. "No, no. I want him hurtin'. And bad! Killing is too easy. One shot and he's out of it. I want the lousy son of a bitch to hurt!" He raised his somber eyes to the earthen roof. "Like me. I want him hurtin' like me!" He lowered his head and his eyes stared wildly at Chiverton.

"But I . . ."

"He's going to pay for Carl. And he is not going only to pay for that poor boy in spades, but with the whole of the fucking deck!"

"For Carl!" Chiverton was totally staggered at the words he was hearing. "But I thought . . ."

"A lot of people thought!" snapped Bruin. "On account of I let them. They thought I didn't give a shit in hell for Carl. But listen to me, you whippersnapper: Carl Bruin was Harry Bruin's brother! My brother! And that son of a bitch lying right there killed him. You hear me, Slocum! You killed Harry Bruin's brother! You are going to pay for that—and slowly! Real slowly!"

Lying face down on the floor of the root cellar, Slocum heard Harry Bruin. He didn't move. He didn't change his breathing. His head felt as though it had been broken, but he didn't make a sound. And he could hear Harry Bruin.

He had known it would come to that. Not Carl. Not Carl Bruin. But Harry Bruin's brother.

9

He must have passed out again, for the next thing he knew he had opened his eyes in the pitch dark. He was still lying face down on the dirt floor, where Harry Bruin's pistol barrel had driven him. His head was splitting; his eyes felt as though they were being squeezed in a vise. Slowly, he brought himself around and began to focus into the dark.

Slowly he moved, feeling now the stickiness on the back of his head. He heard the door open and the beam of a lantern lighted the far wall of the room as somebody entered. The light was now spreading all around. He closed his eyes. Bruin again? Chiverton, or Felix, maybe?

He heard a rustling sound and a woman's voice said, "Are you all right?"

He opened his eyes and looked up at Annie. Only it was a different Annie. Her face was cut and bruised, her lips swollen. She had been beaten. Kneeling, she set the lantern beside him and helped him sit up.

"Bruin?" he asked, taking a closer look at her.

"Sweet Harry. And you?"

"His pistol. Shit take it, it's my fault he did it to you."

"I'm glad you told him."

"No. I did it to make him mad."

"Well, you succeeded." She tried to grin, but it was too painful. "Look, I don't hold that against you. You had every right to tell him anything to get out of here. And Harry's always had a temper, a hell of a temper, since I've known him."

He sat straighter now, feeling himself gingerly for further damage. Then he looked at her again. "I'm really sorry."

Again she tried to smile, but it hurt her mouth. Yet she was holding him with her eyes. "Want to know something, Slocum?"

"What?"

"It was worth it. Oh God, it was worth it." She closed her eyes for a moment and opened them again."

"I'll take your word for it," Slocum said, tenderly feeling the back of his head. Then he grinned at her, seeing the seriousness in her face. Suddenly she reminded him of a little girl. "I think it was worth it too," he said gently. And he put his arm around her.

She looked down. When he touched the side of her head she leaned against him and he could tell she was crying. But it lasted only a moment.

She leaned away from him, dabbing at her eyes,

and said, "Sorry. I'm sorry." Then she had control of herself and sat up straight, away from him.

"We've got to get you out of here," she said.

"And you?"

"Me? I don't know about that."

"Has he beaten you before?"

"Oh, yeah. Harry's not the most gentle lover in the world. He likes it . . . certain ways. But let's not talk about it." She had been speaking with her eyes down, and now she looked at him directly. "You treat me decent. I'm not much used to that."

"Well, maybe it breaks the monotony."

They both had a short, painful laugh at that.

"Do you know anything about a woman named Loretta Barclay?"

"Is that the one Chiverton was going to bring out here?"

He nodded.

"I don't know. They were arguing, Harry and Chiverton. Seems she changed her mind or something. I dunno."

"So she didn't come out."

"No. I had the feeling Clay didn't want her coming out anyway, and I think Harry was pretty sore at him. Chiverton's afraid of Harry. Like a lot of people." She paused, touching her lip with her fingers. "Harry was real mad. It was after that he beat me again."

Slocum didn't say anything. He reached out and touched her face softly with his fingers.

She turned her head and kissed his thumb. "Thank you."

"Can you get me out of here without Harry beating you up again?"

She didn't answer, but rose to her feet, reaching

under her shawl. "You can get through that door." She nodded toward the sealed door across the room as she held up a key. "Harry can be managed, so don't worry. It depends on how hungry he is."

He studied her a moment and then he said, "It leads outside?"

She nodded. "It might take a bit to open it. They sealed it as much as they could. Anyhow, I brought this, just in case." This time she brought forth a buffalo-skinning knife and handed it to him.

It didn't take long to get the door open. The buffalo knife served to dig out the sealing. The door came open with a grinding sound.

"I'll wish you good luck then," she said.

"You're not coming?"

She shook her head.

"What about Harry? And him?" He nodded toward the other door.

"I can handle Harry; and that son of a bitch out there too."

He waited, looking down at her corn-silk hair as she stood there with her head bowed. Then she looked up at him.

"You just follow the passage through. It comes out in a stand of cottonwoods down by a creek. Not far from the corral. You're on your own then, Slocum."

He still waited. "One question: Do you know anything about Bruin planning to take over Medicine Fork?"

"They're getting ready right now. That's how come I got in here. They're all busy as hell getting ready. I heard Harry say they'd be riding tomorrow."

"Know how many men he's got?"

"A lot. I'd guess at least twenty, maybe twenty-five. Maybe even more."

"You sure you don't want to come along?"

"Love is a funny thing, ain't it," she said, and it seemed to him that she didn't even realize what she was doing as her fingers touched the big bruise on her cheek.

But Slocum did know what he was doing when he reached out and ran his big hand gently through her hair.

Then he was gone through the door.

He still had matches, enough light to see the fallen timbers, some lying directly across the narrow passageway. There were others supporting rather dangerously the roof under which he made his way. The whole tunnel was busy with rats, and he wondered how long the timbers that had remained standing would support the passage. It was only a moment, though, before he stepped into a wider area and could feel a slight current of air on his hands and face.

Was it an old mining shaft? he wondered. Maybe. Yet there was little rock or anything that might have suggested a mining environment. As he moved slowly across the widened area, which was only about twenty feet, he smelled fresh manure, and there suddenly on the ground were droppings. Horse? Maybe mule or burro. He thought of old Charlie the prospector at the same moment that his eyes fell onto the panniers in the corner of what now appeared to be a small room. There was also some rolled bedding, but no sign of the burro or the old man.

Crossing swiftly to the panniers, he opened one.

Inside he felt rocks. He was almost at his last match, but from the feel of the rock, even though he couldn't see it and didn't want to light his matches just yet in case he needed them later, he was sure it was an ore sample.

Slocum stood there in the dark thinking of Charlie and what he could be doing with Bruin. It was pretty damned obvious now that the prospector had been checking on some old mine or a vein of metal for Bruin. Maybe he'd already found it. But it was clear now why Bruin had been playing his kind of hand. He had bigger fish to fry than cattle; at least, he seemed to think so. Or—and this was a thought— why not both? Why not cattle as well as a silver strike? He could take over the town in time for the railroad's arrival, and if there was a big strike announced people would flock and he'd control Medicine Fork with even bigger profit.

And yet there was something missing, he felt. Something wasn't right. It made sense, what he'd figured; but it didn't fit what he knew of Harry Bruin's character. Such a plan was something for maybe a Chiverton—provided he had the guts. Harry Bruin's style was closer to the knuckle. A leopard didn't change his spots. Harry was a born outlaw, not an entrepreneur. Or was he?

He decided to strike one of his final three matches and look at the rock he was holding when he heard something. Swiftly he placed the rock back in the pannier and moved back down the tunnel. Someone was approaching.

In the next instant he heard Chiverton's slippery voice.

"I'll see you tomorrow, then. You've got what

you're going to do. You understand it?"

"Ride Jilly into town and let 'em find out I struck it rich in one of them old shafts." Charlie's voice was bland, like that of a bored child reciting a lesson.

"How are you going to do that?" Chiverton's voice was insistent.

"I drop a hint here and there. Looking for a bank, but too bad there ain't one in town. That kind of thing."

"Right. Right. You do it real easy. You don't *tell* anybody you made a strike. You pretend it's something real small. Leftovers. Thing is, you let them say it. Let *them* discover the big silver strike."

"Gotcha."

"You sure?"

"Jesus," whispered the old prospector.

"Charlie, I don't want any slips. Mr. Bruin doesn't want any slips."

There was a pause now, and Slocum imagined the old prospector taking in the threat. "I gotcha," he said finally.

"You have got what you need out here?"

"I carry it with me, whatever I got need for," responded the crusty old-timer. "Shit, I ain't been livin' in these here hills and mountains all this time with Jilly without the one of us known' something, for Christ's sake!"

"Good enough." Chiverton's last words were sour.

Slocum listened to his receding footsteps, and hugged the wall of the passageway. Charlie walked in carrying a storm lantern and picked up one of the panniers. He merely glanced at it, without inspecting its contents, and in a few moments was gone.

Slocum waited. So that was it—fake silver strike.

Clever. With the town all charged up with the promise of the mines coming back, it would be that much easier to take over, and if Harry had title to the mining area they would have to come to him. And if there wasn't any silver? Simple. Nobody had actually told them there was. Their own greed had led them into the hole. Mr. Bruin would lead them out.

Except it wasn't Harry. It couldn't be. It was Chiverton. Chiverton's idea, Chiverton's plan; the land grants with the mining and railhead as bait. But Harry had taken it over. Harry Bruin had his gang together. And—yes, by God—where there were miners and cattlemen and cowboys and gold and silver seekers, there was booty. It would be the old days of the outlaw trail. Harry was letting Chiverton operate his plan, but he, Harry Bruin, was running the bigger plan. He was going to rob them all blind, and then get out.

Now, as he moved to the end of the tunnel, the air was stronger on him. He stepped out into the open night. It was still dark, though the stars were fading high above him, and it would soon be dawn. It would also bring the whole camp awake, and so he had to work fast.

As he stood by the creek, smelling the water, he realized that if he was going to take Lime and Le-Franc it had to be now. There was no time to ride into town to warn Spider of the impending fake silver strike, followed by the invasion of Harry Bruin's gang. He did have a day, at least, and everything now pointed to Yellow Horse.

He studied the sky, judging it a good two hours till daylight. Thank God he was out of that root cellar. He wondered how Annie was. Had anyone caught her?

It didn't take him long to locate the big horse corral. He waited, studying the layout. He had to have everything working just right. First he found a lariat rope, then saddle rigging. He picked two halters for the horses his prisoners would ride, and a good strong bridle for himself. And he also picked up some pigging string while he was at it. It would definitely come in handy. He was hoping that the guards had not taken a notion to check the root cellar. Surely there would have been an outcry if they had. He was hoping too that Lime and Felix were still at their posts.

He walked into the corral and picked out two horses, besides his spotted pony, leading each outside to the shelter of the cottonwoods, where he saddled them. Then he moved quickly around the cutbank and began slowly approaching the figure he could make out near the door of the old root cellar.

He took a while closing in on the seated figure. Was it still Felix or Jake? He was up against it if not. Stopping every few feet to check for sound, smell, movement, even change in atmosphere, he crept closer. In moments that seemed longer than they actually were, he was right behind the dozing sentry.

"Don't move!" His words were as sharp as the point of the buffalo-skinning knife that he prodded into the man's kidney.

The figure tightened in fear and anger.

"One sound and I carve your kidney right out of your body!"

He heard his prisoner swallow, and his breathing coming faster. Reaching down with his free hand, Slocum drew the other man's sixgun, checked it as best he could without easing up on his prisoner, then shoved it into his belt.

"Where's your partner?"

"Don't got no partner."

He recognized the voice of Felix LeFranc. "I said, where is the other guard?" He jabbed the point of the knife.

LeFranc gasped. "Yonder."

"Who is he?"

"Jake."

He was holding the knife in his left hand, keeping the right free; now he drew Felix's gun from his belt, a big Navy Colt and slammed it down on the back of the guard's head.

The wolfer sagged. Leaning down, Slocum checked him. Then, removing the unconscious man's hat and jacket, he put them on, dragged LeFranc away from where he'd been sitting, and sat down in his place; just in time. The step was heavy and coming from his right side.

"I got coffee." It was Lime's voice, low to fit the dark night.

When there was no answer, Lime said, "Felix, you there?"

Slocum grunted, trying to sound like the wolfer, and even growled a little, as though grumbling from being awakened.

But Lime was sharp. In the dim light Slocum saw him move and heard the whisper of a sixgun clearing leather. In a flash he had leaped across the intervening space and had the skinning knife at Jake Lime's throat. With his other hand he had grabbed the gun, which the astonished Lime released instantly.

"Son of a bitch! Who are ya?"

"You got one guess."

"Slocum—you bastard!"

"Save the compliments. And listen! You and Le-Franc and me are taking a little ride. We will be on horseback but close enough to shake hands. You will do exactly what I tell you. If you don't I won't kill you; I will just cut your balls off. Got it?" He waited a moment for it to sink in.

"Got it." Lime's voice was husky under the point of the buffalo knife.

"That goes for both of you. Even if one fucks up, I'll cut both of you anyway. Remember that!"

He could feel the vibration of Lime's knees shaking.

A groan told him that Felix was coming around. With the gun in one hand and the knife in the other, he pushed Lime over toward his pal. "Get him up. Tell him what I just told you. Remember, if one of you does one thing—even thinks of it—you'll both pay. And remember you will not enjoy the pleasure of getting killed."

Lime gargled something in assent and began helping LeFranc to his feet.

In a few moments they were at the corral and had mounted the three horses.

"There a guard at the end of the canyon?" Slocum asked.

"There is."

He had expected it to be so, but he asked the question just to see how his prisoners would respond. Satisfied that they were sufficiently scared, he ordered them to move ahead of him. After they had ridden partway up the trail to the rimrocks, he told them to dismount and with the pigging string he tied their hands in front of them. They then proceeded on foot, leading their mounts.

As the sky began to lighten, he wondered how long it would take them to get to the Indian camp. Annie had said Bruin was planning to attack the town tomorrow. That gave him this day and a night.

In the timber and in the coulees there were elk and mule deer and pronghorn antelope. There were few buffalo. In the Indian horse herd the colts were lively, trying their spindly new legs, charging into their mothers and staggering about. And in the air came the gentle tinkle of the grazing bells. It was good, the old people said, good to see the land under the nourishing sun, good to see and smell, to experience the new life. Still, there was care in their wording, for the times in general were hard. The blue-coat soldiers were all around, the whites.

Still, there had been no fighting with the pony soldiers for a while, and the white cow people had not done anything bad. The one bad thing had been the shooting of Runs Quickly. A new sorrow had fallen for the fear was that the shooting, though not fatal, had been only a beginning of fresh atrocities, fresh treachery. Stone and his circle of followers had sworn revenge on the whites, and only the stature of Yellow Horse, himself a warrior who could pony whip any young buck into line if necessary, had kept them from attacking the whites.

Now, just at the end of the Moon of the Shedding Colts, the Shoshone, only one sleep away from the nearest whiteskins, were hoping for peace. The young men still smoldered for revenge, but Yellow Horse and his headmen had insisted that it was foolhardy to fight the whites. There were too many. Yellow Horse had received news of Stone's attack on the wagon train during the storm, and he had punished him, removing him from one of the councils.

Thus the band of Yellow Horse minded their own business, going out for meat because there was nothing coming from the agency, and it had been a long, hard winter. Now, with the moon growing again, the land already singing with new life, the elders hoped for a big hunt that would feed the tribe, and would ease the restlessness of the young warriors.

The day had broken gently over the Shoshone camp, the sun touching the tipis, washing over the cottonwood trees and the crackwillow in the coulees that ran through the tawny-colored prairie. Next year, the old ones were saying; next year there would be fewer buffalo, fewer game to fill the parfleches. Some, such as Yellow Horse, looked toward the other world.

As Slocum and his two prisoners rode in toward the Shoshone camp, the wind was stroking the deep grass, causing it to shimmer under the sparkling morning sun. Slocum felt the heat moving into his shoulders, then down along his neck, onto his thighs and the backs of his hands.

Now, as they entered the camp, a group of boys who had been playing the game called Throwing Them Off Their Horses—but using other boys as "horses"—stopped and stared at the interesting caravan. The silence was everywhere as eyes followed every move.

In the chief's lodge, Slocum found Yellow Horse sitting with his headmen. He had entered the lodge carefully, after turning over his prisoners to the camp police, and had seated himself in the place that had been left open for him. He always appreciated how the Indians knew well ahead when a visitor was approaching.

They had smoked and now a silence fell, an interval while inner preparation continued.

"You have brought the men who shot Runs Quickly," Yellow Horse said finally. "It is good."

"I do not know which one," Slocum said.

The chief said nothing, and Slocum did not pursue the matter. He knew the Shoshone would find out.

"Yellow Horse, I have brought these white men to Shoshone justice. Even though according to white man's law I should have taken them to the soldiers."

"That I know, Slocum. I know something of the white man's law. Nothing would have been done."

"And so I have broken the white man's law."

The chief nodded in the heavy silence that surrounded Slocum's words.

"I have something to ask you in return."

"I have been waiting to hear what that is," Yellow Horse said. He looked at his headmen. "We were waiting for you, and we know you have something to say."

"The bad men I told you about, the ones who tried to injure the wagon train."

"The gray men."

"Yes. They are going to attack the houses at Medicine Fork tomorrow. Probably in the early morning."

"What about the soldiers? Can they not help you?" one of the headmen asked.

"The soldiers are very far away. They would never get here on time." Slocum paused. "I know what you are thinking—that you would be in trouble with the army, the soldier men, if you fought even against the gray men."

"That is true," another headman said. "That is the way the whites see everything."

"But I have a plan. You can listen to it." He looked at Yellow Horse, who said nothing. Yet it was in his waiting silence that Slocum knew the chief and his headmen had agreed to hear him.

Slocum waited just another moment, watching the old men shooing away the flies with their eagle-wing fans and buffalo tails which they flicked through the air.

"It is not that I am asking you to fight them, for I know one thing—that you have few guns. Only for hunting. And not many cartridges. But you could come there. You have a large band of men, Yellow Horse. You could come. I have a plan that could work." He paused, looking carefully at the headmen, and then again at Yellow Horse. "I brought you the two wolfers. You know my tongue is straight and my heart is one. I have thought of a good plan."

A silence fell now and lasted several beats. The Indians sat motionless.

Then Yellow Horse picked up his small clay pipe and lighted it. Some of the other headmen followed suit, tamping in the tobacco and lighting up with the chip taken from the small fire around which they were sitting. The pipes guttered lightly in the new silence.

Yellow Horse spoke then. "There is the fight with Stone. The trouble between you. Will you fight him?"

The chief's words surprised Slocum. He hadn't been thinking of Stone, and had no idea that Stone's hatred for him had reached to Yellow Horse and his council. But of course, he realized now, the chief would know everything that went on. And there was

Silent Flower. He knew that the chief was concerned. Somehow Yellow Horse's words caught him in surprise, and he almost smiled, appreciating once again the subtlety of the Indian's mind.

"Stone wants to fight me? I will fight him. He has no reason to fight me, Yellow Horse. It is that his heart is sick. But I will fight him. It is a matter of honor for all concerned."

"Heya," said the headmen. "It is good."

Yellow Horse stood up. "It will be so."

They had stripped to the waist, both lean, sinewy, quick, with their bodies completely in control. Stone was thicker in body than Slocum, and heavier. His size was unusual for an Indian. Slocum had realized how Stone's hatred for him had affected the whole band. Something had to be settled, and he saw how Yellow Horse understood these subtle needs of his people. The chief knew that Stone was being foolish, had no cause for dispute, yet realized at the same time that the Shoshone's anger was poisoning him and could even spread into a dissatisfaction amongst others. It was better to have everything out in the open, and a matter of honor settled once and for all.

But Slocum had reached an agreement with the chief and his headmen while still back in Yellow Horse's lodge. It would be foolish for either of them to kill the other. Slocum had no reason or need to kill Stone. Why eliminate a good man who could be useful to the tribe for many more years? He had argued that they bend toward the white man's way in this instance and go for a "defeat," where the opponent would be at the point of death, helpless, but not killed.

Yellow Horse and his headmen had not agreed at first, but then Slocum had pointed out how such a defeat would be even greater, for the loser would have to live with it, denying himself the luxury of death. Finally, Yellow Horse and his headmen had agreed. After all, warriors were not easy to come by, warriors who had had the old training, for now the new, younger ones were denied the old ways and were less than those who had fought the soldiers and had hunted the buffalo. And they had agreed. And so had Stone. The death stroke would be withheld. Stone had taken some convincing, but he had finally realized the subtlety of such a defeat, where the loser would have to live for the rest of his life with his failure. There was no doubt in his mind as to the outcome.

These thoughts flashed through Slocum's mind as he stepped into the circle to face Stone. Everyone was there, the circle being held by the camp police who with their pony whips kept the eager ones back, not to allow them to crowd the combatants. Slocum wondered if Silent Flower was present among the women. But the thought was gone almost before it struck him, for here was Stone. Stone with that big, razor-edged buffalo knife in his hand.

Yellow Horse stood now between them, giving instructions, saying that wounding was allowed, but that the death stroke would be withheld. There was muttering amongst the spectators at his words, but no one raised his voice. It was obviously something of the white man's way, and who could ever understand the ways of the white man?

Stone had begun circling around Slocum with the big skinning knife in his right hand. He was slightly crouched and beneath his satin skin his muscles moved like snakes.

It was very hot in the meadow, but neither combatant felt the sun bearing down on his bare back. All at once the Indian sprang forward, his knife sweeping an arc toward Slocum's belly. Reversing the stroke, he raised the blade and a murmur went up from the onlookers as a streak of red appeared on Slocum's upper arm. Fortunately, Slocum had been moving away, and so the wound was superficial.

Slocum kept on circling, letting Stone take the offense. The Shoshone now darted in, and immediately sprang back; again he feinted, ducked, bobbed and weaved. Slocum circled in such a way that he was always facing the Indian.

Now again Stone struck with his blade, waist-high, and Slocum felt the point of the knife strike along the top of his trousers. Swiftly he slashed at the Indian's shoulder and saw a thin pencil line of blood. Stone stepped back, half tripping, and Slocum drove in and their knife arms locked in mid-air. At the same time Stone grabbed Slocum around the waist, while Slocum's free arm circled the Indian's head. Locked together, they kept on their feet, struggling for the upper hand. All at once Slocum kicked his heel against Stone's ankle and they were on the ground, still locked together, neither letting loose his grip as they rolled.

Stone sank his teeth into Slocum's neck, and when the white man loosened his grip, the Indian broke free. His big fist slammed down on Slocum's wrist and he rolled up to his feet. Slocum was on his knees, Stone's blow having made him drop his knife.

A cry went up from the crowd of onlookers. Stone

had the white man now. He could have claimed victory. But it was too much for Stone. He charged, slashing with his knife; the blade cut the air only where Slocum had been. It was clear that Stone was going to kill.

The crowd was roaring as the fight heated up so unexpectedly. But Stone's treachery had charged Slocum with a fresh energy. Now, as the Indian charged again, he ducked the flashing blade, dropped to the ground, and kicked as hard as he could right into the Indian's crotch. Stone staggered, his jaw sagging with pain, and fell to his knees. He was still clutching his knife. Slocum had rolled over, grabbed his own fallen knife, and was rising now as the Indian bore in on him again. He slashed. The blade cut right along the Indian's neck. Stone fell back, dropping his knife, and Slocum was on top of him, the point of his blade just inches away from his opponent's throat. Stone was finished.

A great silence fell on the watching group as the combatants picked themselves up and faced Yellow Horse.

"Your treachery failed you," the chief said, speaking slowly with his eyes on Stone. "You would have killed the white man, but he in his turn spared you. He could have killed you and did not. You will live with that shame for the rest of your days." He waited, letting his words sink in, while Stone remained before him with his head down. At last Yellow Horse turned to the assembled people.

"It is enough," he said.

As the people dispersed he turned to Slocum. "I will help you with your plan. I could not do otherwise."

10

The first person Slocum saw when he rode into Medicine Fork was the girl Loretta. She had just come out of McHenry's General Store, carrying a large bundle. Slocum swung down from his horse and ground-hitched him.

"Can I help you with that bundle, lady?"

To his astonishment, she smiled at him. "Thank you, Marshal."

He took it from her, catching the smell of perfume, just slight but enough to affect him. Before he could say anything she was speaking.

"I want to apologize for being rather rude to you when you warned me about . . . about that man."

"Chiverton."

"Yes. It developed that he was hardly a gentleman."

"Better to find those things out late than never."

She was looking at him in a strange way. "Well, anyway, I did want to apologize." Flushing suddenly all over her face, she reached out and took the bundle from him. "I can manage, Marshal Slocum. Thank you." And she was gone. But something was different, Slocum told himself; something was very definitely different.

He didn't follow. He felt something singing inside him, and that was enough for the moment. Besides, he had a big job ahead. Loretta Barclay would have to wait.

At the other end of town a crowd was gathered. Slocum walked quickly toward it to see what was happening. About a dozen men were standing around a sign that said ELECT WILFONG FOR MAYOR. As he got closer he could hear the voice of the candidate.

"You see this here cigar stub, right? I'll bet you think this is just a ordinary cigar butt that Phineas P. Wilfong smoked maybe only last night." Pause. "But you would be wrong." The amber eyes bored into the listeners, not turning toward Slocum at all as he approached. "You would be dead wrong, 'cause this ain't no ordinary cigar at all. This here . . ." He held the unlighted butt aloft so that everyone could see. "This here is the cigar that General Ulysses S. Grant was smoking just a hour before he accepted the surrender of Robert E. Lee!" Pause. "Now you just think about that. I personally have taken four short puffs of this cigar. Four!" He held up four fingers for everybody to see. "And I am now offering this famous cigar—a pure Havana tobacco, let me hasten to add—for auction. Now, we need money for the campaign, so we're going to raise it by auctioning off some of my fabulous collection of memorabilia from famous folks. Like this here!" He raised his arm aloft, holding the cigar carefully. "Who'll start the bidding? Do I hear ten dollars? Ten?"

"I'll bid four bits," somebody shouted from the back row.

"There is always one in every crowd," said Spider Wilfong, looking gloomily at Slocum, who had pushed his way to the front.

"Better break it up, folks. We got business coming up," Slocum said, lifting his voice. He took the startled Wilfong by the arm and began leading him away. A shout of nervous laughter followed them down the street.

"What the hell you doing!" Spider snarled, pulling his arm away from Slocum. "You be the law, but not on me!"

"Shut up. I want to talk to you. Bruin's going to be riding in here sooner than I want to think about."

"So what?"

"So this. He'll have about twenty-some guns riding with him. Now, let's get into your office and I want you to listen. Just shut up and listen!" He had stopped at the door of a rickety shack, Spider's office, and now he turned the knob and walked in. The man who would be mayor of Medicine Fork followed him with his jaw hanging open. For one of the few times in his life, Phineas Wilfong was speechless.

And he remained virtually speechless during the twenty minutes and upwards that it took John Slocum to relate his plan.

When Slocum was finally finished, Spider let a

huge sigh run through his small body. "Holy Moses!"

Slocum took out a quirly and lighted it.

"Slocum, you figure that'll work? It is one crazy, crazier'n hell plan! I mean, crazy. . .!"

Slocum lifted his Stetson hat and readjusted it on his head. "It'll work. It will work because it has got to work." He had started toward the door. "And I will be wanting a bonus for saving you and Medicine Fork, Mr. Wilfong."

On his way out the door he narrowly missed crashing into Preacher Chimes who, startled out of some daydream or other, was so completely thrown by his narrow escape that in his confusion he blessed the sheriff of Medicine Fork.

In the thin gray light before the dawn the column rode heavily toward the town. During the night there had been a light rainfall, and now the land smelled fresh and new. In the far peaks of the western mountains the light began to gather in preparation for the sunrise.

At the head of the column of twenty riders Harry Bruin rode his big dappled gray horse. Beside him Clay Chiverton kept not quite abreast, careful about his distance as always.

"We'll make it in good time," Bruin said. "Just as the sun hits 'em. Coming in from the east, and they'll have it in their eyes."

Chiverton nodded. He felt chilly in the early morning and tightened his shoulders. His eyes dropped down to his Wellington boots. He had shined them just the night before. "Shouldn't have any trouble," he said. "All they've got is a few Henrys and some handguns."

"Thing is we'll scare 'em," Bruin said sagely. "Early morning's the best time to take a town." He spat reflectively to one side, not caring at all that he was upwind of his fellow rider with the fancy boots, and not seeing that some spittle sprayed onto that new shine.

Chiverton kicked his own horse away from the dappled gray and its rider. He was furious, and more so when he saw that Bruin didn't even notice.

"And noon ain't bad neither," Harry Bruin continued.

"Noon?"

"Towns are sleepy at noon. Course, dawn's better. Before they're up and about. They're still in their sleep, or maybe screwing—one."

It was the simplest of plans. They would ride in with the brilliant sunrise at their backs, making it hard for anyone who might be up to see them. They would have the full advantage of surprise and the fact that the town was still asleep. Surprise and mostly shock, was how Bruin had explained it when he'd mapped the strategy.

Now the outlaw leader raised his fist and pumped it above his head as he kicked his horse into a canter. In a moment, as the sun burst behind them, he signaled the column to fan out. Now they were spread out in a line galloping down onto the sleeping town. The men, already instructed in the procedure, had their guns out. When Bruin fired his first shot, all began shooting as they came pounding into the little one-street town. The houses rattled under the hail of gunfire, and tents were ripped. Some men had drawn rein to slash guy ropes and tents began collapsing. They raced through and around the town, turned their horses and began racing back.

Suddenly Harry Bruin pulled up at the edge of town, raising his arm and shouting at the top of his lungs, "Stop firing! Stop firing!"

The last shot fired into the strange silence that enveloped the town and the marauding riders.

"What the hell's the matter?" cried Chiverton. "There's nobody firing back!"

It was true. Not a single shot had been fired in return.

Harry Bruin sat the frisky dappled gray, reloading his handgun. "Son of a bitch! Looks to me like they ain't nobody in the fuckin' town!"

"They could be hiding," somebody said. "Layin' for us."

"We'll sure as hell find out. Cole, you go down that side of the street, and Dutch, you take th'other. Split the men, ten each side. The rest of you stick with me."

The horses and riders were milling in surprise and agitation at the totally unexpected reaction of the townspeople.

"Sons of bitches could of took plumb off!" snarled Harry Bruin. "How the hell they got word?" He glared malevolently at Chiverton. "That bitch Annie, you think?"

Chiverton's astonishment had driven the color right out of his face. "I don't know."

"What *do* you know, for Christ's sake?"

"They ain't here." Chiverton pointed to the men coming out of the first building, and now those coming out of another building. They were shaking their heads.

"You're a goddamn bright son of a bitch, Chiverton, my boy. Figurin' that out!"

Still furious, Clay Chiverton had taken a moment to lean down and wipe the spittle off his Wellington boot.

"Search everywhere!" Bruin shouted. "The bastards could be hiding. They could backshoot us, for Christ's_sake! The livery. Look in the livery!" He sat his horse right in the middle of the street. In the distance now they all heard the locomotive whistle.

"Track's coming closer," Chiverton observed.

"Shut up!" Bruin spat furiously over his horse's withers and scratched himself behind his knee. "Where the hell do you reckon the buggers went to? There is nothin' out there but prairie and weather!"

Suddenly a shout went up. Bruin followed the rider's pointing finger.

"Over yonder!"

All heads turned now, as the searchers who had about finished their task began riding back to their leader. He was standing up in his stirrups staring in total disbelief at what they were all now seeing.

A long, long line, making almost a circle around the town; a line of men on horseback and foot was approaching quickly.

"There they be, by God!" someone shouted gleefully, and fired his gun in the air.

"Stop that!" shouted Bruin. "Take a look behind them, for Christ's sake!"

Chiverton's jaw had dropped open. "God almighty!"

Ringed behind the inhabitants of Medicine Fork were Shoshone warriors in full battle regalia. They raced their horses back and forth behind the line of whites who were rapidly bearing down on the town. They remained behind the leaders who were now within firing range and still hadn't fired a shot. Suddenly they stopped, and as Bruin and his gang watched, a man detached himself from the group—a man on a spotted horse. It was Slocum who now galloped toward them.

Swift as a snake, Clay Chiverton had raised his Sharps carbine and sighted. Even more swiftly, Harry Bruin had laid the barrel of his .44 across his pupil's knuckles. The Sharps clattered to the ground.

"You asshole!" Bruin almost spat the words into the pain-filled face of Chiverton. "They got more Injuns out there than whipped Custer, for Christ's sake. Don't you got a brain in yer head?"

Half a dozen riders had detached themselves from the circle of whites and Indians and were following Slocum.

"They have got us surrounded," Chiverton said, his face pale with fury.

"We'll make a break for the Hole!" shouted Harry Bruin, and kicked his horse.

But almost in the same moment, Slocum, who had been riding in fast, watching Bruin and Chiverton with the attention of an eagle watching its prey, suddenly drew rein. Lifting the Winchester he had been carrying in his left hand, he took aim and fired.

Harry Bruin's dappled gray let out a scream and fell to his knees. The rider tumbled head over heels, ending up on his back.

In the same instant the men with Slocum began firing, and those behind them booted their horses in toward the town and the outlaws who, without their brash, furious leader, were uncertain about which way to go. Their hesitancy was costly, and was all the townspeople needed. They galloped in, firing with telling accuracy, accompanied by the Shoshone;

not so many of them, for they hadn't many weapons. Yet the shock of their appearance and the effectiveness of the bullets and arrows they did have made short work of the gunmen bunched around Harry Bruin, who had twisted his ankle, and Clay Chiverton. Chiverton threw down his gun and raised his hands.

Pulling up right where Bruin was still lying on the ground clutching an empty sixgun, Slocum held up his hand to cease fire.

As he did so, Bruin's men threw down their guns.

"Let 'em fight it out theirselves," one man muttered, and he could have been saying it for the whole group.

Clay Chiverton lowered his hands slowly, his wary eyes on Slocum. "There's the man who's been wanting to kill you, Slocum." He nodded toward the man on the ground, who was trying to stand, but his ankle again gave out.

"Damn! Old age finally got to me! But you, you dirty little son of a bitch. If I had a bullet in this gun, I'd sure as hell finish you!" He let the sixgun fall at his side as he twisted around to face Chiverton.

Suddenly, without warning, he spat a long streak of tobacco juice and a small lump of tobacco right onto Chiverton's boots.

Slocum watched Chiverton's hand striking toward his hideout, which Slocum had by no means forgotten. But the unarmed Harry Bruin was quicker. In a flash he had seized the gun that he himself had dropped only moments before, leveled it, and shot Clay Chiverton right in the chest.

Harry's shot knocked the gun out of the outlaw's hand. Harry was grinning. He was laughing as he

watched the astonishment in his pupil's face while
Chiverton sank to the ground, dying.

"It—it was loaded," he gasped, his eyes bugging
at the gun that Bruin had dropped. "You said, you
said . . ."

Harry Bruin was shaking with laughter. "You forgot lesson number two," he said. "You forgot, you
dumb shit, that a gun is *always* loaded!"

It took the rest of the morning for the town to get
settled down after the heady action of the early
hours. Slocum was pleased. They had all followed
his plan just as he had outlined it.

After the shooting of Clay Chiverton, and when
the wounded had been attended to—three outlaws,
and one townsman who had shot himself in the foot
—Slocum found himself sitting quietly in his office.
He had ordered the outlaws out of the country now
and forever, and he locked Harry Bruin in Bruin's
own "office" at the edge of town, leaving a guard on
duty.

"You'll be turned over to the law, I reckon," he
had told the old outlaw when he padlocked him in the
shed behind the office.

Bruin had grinned at him. "Like wearing tin, do
you, Slocum?"

"You like wearing that chain?"

Slocum had nodded at the chain that was holding
his prisoner to the wall. "You take off with that,
you'll be dragging the shack with you," he observed
sardonically.

He had just lighted a quirly when there was a
knock on the door and it opened to admit Annie.

"Mind if I come in?"

"Have a seat," he said, swinging his legs off the table and onto the floor.

"I guess you know why I've come."

She seated herself on an upturned crate facing him. She looked tired and drawn, but he still felt the excitement for her, and he could see she felt it too.

"I reckon you'd do anything for that, for me to let him go."

She sighed, nodded. "I know. You're a lawman and you've got your duty. But if I guarantee to get him plumb out of the country...would you...?" Her eyes, her whole posture entreated him as she leaned forward.

"I just resigned this job as of about an hour ago," Slocum said. "So, actually, you'll have to talk to the new law."

"Who would that be?" she asked, sitting back in surprise.

"Dunno. But meanwhile, there is the mayor."

"The mayor?"

"Spider Wilfong."

Her face went blank then as she whispered, "Holy shit."

Slocum couldn't help the slow grin that appeared in his face. "Kind of funny, wouldn't you say?"

She nodded. It was something in the way she nodded, or so he told himself afterwards when he thought about it, when it was all over and there was time to think. But somehow his body now knew something his head didn't yet know. He was on his feet as the sound came at the door, but he knew it wasn't the door, for he had already spun to the window of the little office, his hand striking to his holstered gun and drawing and squeezing as Harry

Bruin's shot came right through the window, nicking him in the arm, but in no way denying the ultimate truth of Slocum's bullet. Outside the window of the office, Harry Bruin received Slocum's bullet right between his eyes.

He turned back to the girl. "That was a pretty rotten thing to do," he said.

She didn't drop her eyes, but he saw something change in them. "I told you I loved him. Maybe you didn't hear me."

When Spider Wilfong burst into the room, Slocum was still standing there looking at the girl.

"What happened?" the little man asked, speaking with his British accent for the first time in some while.

"Business for your undertaker, Mayor." Slocum nodded toward the broken window.

Spider was looking at the girl. "Who is this?"

The girl raised her head. She was about to speak but Slocum cut her off. "My sister," he said. "She's from San Francisco. Just passing through."

That night the town celebrated. Slocum had announced his resignation, and Spider Wilfong was still trying to auction off the historical cigar butt of General Ulysses S. Grant, along with other memorabilia. He had a bullet taken from the body of the famous Indian chief Tecumseh, and a pair of spectacles once used by (though not actually owned by) Benjamin Franklin—a touch of "authenticity" that especially delighted Slocum. He had a garter that had formerly encircled one of the shapely legs of the fabled Julia Bulette. The old boy was in special form, and everyone accepted the fact that the election was as good as won.

For Slocum it seemed definitely the right time to move on. Spider had paid him well for his work, and Cassie had added a special dividend in his bedroll. Fun, after all, was the only real payment. Still, there did remain a bit of unfinished business.

As he looked past the group crowded around Spider Wilfong just outside the Good Time Place Saloon and Gaming Hall he saw the piece of unfinished business walking briskly north on the other side of the street. It swept into his mind how different, how very different she'd been when he'd offered to help her with her bundle the other day as she was coming out of McHenry's General Store.

Slocum knew he had nothing to lose; and in fact this day he knew was one of those when he would win. It was so obvious that the general tension that had been building this good while in the town had suddenly evaporated. And so, why not . . . ?

It didn't matter whether it was explained or not. And later, as he held her hand, standing beneath the willow trees that lined the creek south of town, while they both smelled the fresh grass, their horses, the water, and the night sky, he knew he was still winning. The little voice inside him had told him not to hurry away, and it was telling him again now. After all he could leave tomorrow. There was always tomorrow. And after tomorrow . . . there was the next day.

JAKE LOGAN

J.D. HARDIN

"THE MOST EXCITING WESTERN WRITER SINCE LOUIS L'AMOUR"
—JAKE LOGAN

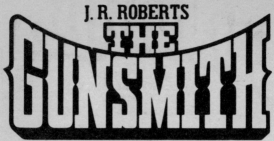

J. R. ROBERTS
THE GUNSMITH
SERIES

Available at your local bookstore or return this form to:

 **CHARTER**
THE BERKLEY PUBLISHING GROUP, Dept. B
390 Murray Hill Parkway, East Rutherford, NJ 07073

Please send me the titles checked above. I enclose _____. Include $1.00 for postage and handling if one book is ordered; add 25¢ per book for two or more not to exceed $1.75. CA, IL, NJ, NY, PA, and TN residents please add sales tax. Prices subject to change without notice and may be higher in Canada.

NAME_____

ADDRESS_____

CITY_____ STATE/ZIP_____

(Allow six weeks for delivery.)   A1